Arctic Fire

Also by Keira Andrews

Arctic Fire

BY KEIRA ANDREWS

Arctic Fire
Written and published by Keira Andrews
Cover by Dar Albert

Copyright © 2016 by Keira Andrews
Print Edition

ISBN: 978-1-988260-10-5

This is a work of fiction. Names, characters, businesses, places, events and incidents are either the products of the author's imagination or used in a fictitious manner. No persons, living or dead, were harmed by the writing of this book. Any resemblance to any actual persons, living or dead, or actual events is purely coincidental.

Acknowledgments

My gratitude to C for sharing his experiences as a gay man in Nunavut. Thanks as well to Anne-Marie, Becky, Mary, and Rachel for the beta reading and encouragement, as always.

Author's Note

While Arctic Bay and Nanisivik are actual places and the Canadian Rangers are real military reservists bravely protecting our North, this is a work of fiction.

Chapter One

"*NUNAVUTMUT TUNNGASUGITSI!*"

Gravel and a thin layer of snow crunched under Jack's boots, and he cursed himself as he stepped onto the runway at the Arctic Bay Airport. He'd completely blanked on learning the basics of Inuktitut. He'd been told most people in Nunavut spoke English as well, but he'd always found a few phrases in the native tongue could go a long way.

He hurried away from the turbo prop plane so he wasn't blocking the handful of passengers behind him. "Thank you," he said with a smile, guessing that the older Inuit man had surely offered some kind of greeting.

Head high, the stout man saluted. "Welcome, Captain Turner. I'm Master Corporal Donald Onartok."

"Good to meet you." He saluted and then shook the man's callused hand, shivering as the wind whipped across the airfield. His nostrils already tingled from the dry, cold air. "No coat?" Jack wore his dark camo parka, which came to mid-thigh over his matching pants.

Onartok waved a hand. "It's only minus seven. Still balmy in October." He wore the Canadian Ranger uniform: black combat boots, camo pants in the same dark pattern as Jack's, red hooded sweatshirt, and red baseball cap—both with insignia. He yanked on a pair of gloves and hitched his thumb over his shoulder. "I'll give you the tour. Won't take long."

The terminal was a small one-story rectangle raised off the ground and painted in gray and light blues. Satellite dishes and antennas pointed to the cloudless sky, and as Jack fell into step, he had to shield his eyes with his hand. The sun reflecting off the snow made it as bright as the desert outside Kabul. "Shouldn't have packed my sunglasses."

"Sun'll be down in an hour or so, but you can get them from your bag before we head off."

Jack checked his multipurpose watch. It was only fifteen hundred, but the sun was indeed sinking toward the horizon. The temperature gauge was in Fahrenheit and read nineteen degrees. "Where's Sergeant Carsen?" He hoped he'd remembered the name correctly from glancing at the briefing package.

"Still at school. He teaches."

"Thanks for coming to get me. What do you do?"

"Hunt and fish." When Onartok smiled, his teeth gleamed and his narrow-set eyes almost disappeared. "You gave me an excuse to take the afternoon off. My wife couldn't argue with going to pick up an army VIP."

Jack resisted the urge to snort. *VIP*. More like a fuck-up the brass didn't know what to do with. Maybe he should have taken early retirement after all. At least he would have avoided ridiculous assignments like this one.

Inside the terminal there were more handshakes and greetings from the handful of people there. Before climbing into Onartok's pickup truck, Jack fished out his sunglasses and gloves from his duffel and double checked that his weapons case was secure.

"This is the only highway in Nunavut," Onartok noted as they turned out of the airport.

Jack blinked at the snow-dusted dirt road, which had no right to be called a highway. "This goes to Nanisivik?"

"That's right. It's the only road in Nunavut connecting two communities. I guess Nanisivik isn't a community no more since no one lives there. It was a company town. That means all the houses and buildings were built by the mine. Dismantled it all when they left."

Jack knew what a company town was, but didn't say so. "They mined lead there, right?"

"And zinc and silver. It was the first mine north

of the Arctic Circle. They closed it in 2002 when the metal prices fell too far. Now it's just the port. The navy was supposed to turn it into a base, but then they changed their minds. Cutbacks, you know. They're still supposed to make it a refueling station for the navy ships in summer, but nothing's happened yet." He laughed nervously. "Sorry. I reckon you already know all this."

"No, no. I want to hear your perspective. From what I understand, the navy plans call for a glorified gas station." The army was hatching plans of its own, of course—plans that would very likely come to nothing, just as the navy's had.

As the curving road came around a cliff, the sparkling bay appeared to the left, and a signpost to the right. It was in English with Inuktitut symbols beneath.

No liquor beyond this point without a permit

Jack sighed internally. He'd been traveling for ten hours, and he'd really been looking forward to a cold beer. He thought of the folder of information on Arctic Bay and Nanisivik that Colonel Fournier had given him, which surely mentioned it was a dry town.

He'd procrastinated all week and promised himself he'd read the briefing on the plane, but he'd slept instead. Considering he'd had a four-hour layover in Iqaluit after the early flight from Ottawa, he had no excuse. Particularly since he'd spent the time playing a stupidly addictive fishing game on his tablet.

But it was fine—he'd get up to speed tonight in his hotel room. It wasn't as though there would be anything else to do. "How many people live here?" he asked, since he should try to make conversation.

"Eight hundred and twenty-three last they counted. But I reckon the number's gone up a bit. I know it has by at least one since my third son was born."

Jack smiled on cue. "Congratulations. What's his name?"

"Ipiktok. It means sharp. Smart, I mean. Brainy."

"That's a good name."

"My wife wanted to go traditional. A lot of babies have old names these days. And Arctic Bay is Ikpiarjuk. It means the pocket. You'll see there are cliffs on three sides."

Beneath the windswept patches of snow, the barren red-rock landscape was hilly and dominated by flat-topped cliffs. Jack couldn't see any vegetation or even topsoil. *Might as well be the fucking moon.*

As the town itself appeared, things didn't improve much. Arctic Bay was a collection of mostly single-story prefabricated houses, many painted light blue or dark red. He guessed there were about a hundred small buildings clustered together by the shore. Walking from one end of town to the other couldn't take more than ten minutes.

"So this is it," Onartok said as they drove down

toward the water. He glanced over expectantly.

"Looks great," Jack lied.

"I'll take you to the hotel, and Sergeant Carsen will be along soon."

Jack smiled and nodded as he took in his home for the next five days. This whole trip was a waste of time, but at least it got him out from behind a desk pushing pointless paper. He'd told himself it would be a welcome break, although it wasn't as if Colonel Fournier had given him a choice.

He could still hear Etienne's disappointed sigh, his mouth turned down as he clasped his hands together on his desk.

"Something needs to give, Jack. I know it's hard to transition. But you seem distracted here. I think it'll do you good to get back in the field."

"Going on a tour with Arctic reservists isn't getting back in the field. They aren't even real army."

"They're all we've got up there, and they know that land. You just might learn something. We're getting out of the Middle East—time to focus closer to home."

But what was the point? If the Russians wanted to invade the Arctic, a few weekend warriors couldn't stop them. Even with the waning sunlight glittering prettily on the partly frozen bay, this place was a wasteland, and a fucking freezing one at that. Ottawa was bad enough, and Jack could only shudder to think what it would be like here on the north end of Baffin Island in the winter.

On the upside, at least there was no goddamned sand.

The Siqiniq Hotel was a wide brown prefab rectangle that couldn't house more than ten tiny rooms. He'd seen fancier mud huts in Afghanistan, but as long as it was clean he didn't care. As Jack climbed out of the truck, he peered at the small posts that lifted the structure a few feet off the ground. He noticed all the buildings were similarly hoisted. "Why is everything lifted?" It was so dry in the high Arctic it couldn't be to prevent flooding.

"Permafrost," Onartok answered as he scooped up Jack's duffel from the back of the pickup. "If buildings sit right on the ground, the heat from inside will melt the top layer. They'll sink."

"Ah. No basements in Nunavut, I guess." Jack reached for his bag and extended his hand. "Thanks again."

"My pleasure, Captain." Onartok shook his hand and nodded. "There's Susan. She'll take good care of you."

A middle-aged woman appeared from the door of the hotel. "This must be Captain Turner. *Tunngasugitsi*. Welcome."

Her dark hair was pulled into a ponytail, and she had the tan skin of most Inuit Jack had met. He followed her inside. She grabbed a key from behind a little front desk area and pointed to a room that opened up off to the right.

"This is the dining room. Dinner will be served starting at six. Breakfast is at seven, and lunch at noon."

Inside there were six square tables with four chairs each and a TV up in the corner. No-smoking signs sat on the shiny metal napkin dispensers. A group of teenagers clustered around a table drinking coffee. They peered at him curiously but said nothing.

Susan led the way down a brightly lit corridor. Jack counted six rooms all together on either side of the hall, and his was at the end. There were two beds across from the door, both narrow doubles with a small bedside table and lamp between them. Susan went to the gold lamp and turned the switch, sending a warm glow over the brown carpet through the lampshade. On the pale oak dresser beside the door to the left sat a flat-screen TV. A bathroom was also to the left.

"Thank you, Susan. This is great." The room was neat and clean, and although a hint of must remained, he suspected it had been aired out earlier in the day. He'd certainly laid his head in far worse places. A memory of a scorpion scuttling across his blanket in a dusty tent in the desert flashed through his mind.

"Would you like coffee?" she asked.

"No, just some water. Can I drink from the tap?"

"Yes, it's safe. There are glasses in the bathroom."

A thought occurred to Jack. "If there's permafrost, where does the water come from?"

Susan went to the window and drew back one side of the heavy burgundy drapes, which were half open. She pointed. "Water tank and sewage tank. The town fills the water and collects the other. The water comes from a lake nearby. Don't worry, it's chlorinated before they put it in the tank."

"No problem."

"We do ask that you try to conserve water and not take long showers. If the water truck breaks down or the driver gets sick, we can run out."

"Of course."

She smiled and backed toward the door. "The wifi password is on the card on the dresser. I hope you enjoy your stay."

He thanked her and dropped his parka on one bed before sitting on the other nearest the bathroom. The mattress felt thick enough, and the bedsprings only creaked a little. The stiff bedspread was mottled pinks and burgundy in a square pattern, and the walls were painted in a pink-toned beige.

Jack went to the window and peered out at what he could see of Arctic Bay, which at this point in the day was shadowed low buildings and lights flickering on. He could only glimpse the bay itself, which was shrouded in darkness now.

The compact bathroom had a toilet, sink and bathtub with shower. Jack rolled up the sleeves of his green combat sweater and splashed his face with water, careful to turn the taps off quickly. He winced at the dark smudges under his eyes.

Any hint of the tan he'd had in Afghanistan was long gone from his pale skin. He dried his face on a thin towel and drank a small glass of water. His short blond hair was sticking up, and he patted it down before giving up. Who the hell was he going to be impressing in this place? Fuck his hair.

On the bed, he pulled the briefing folder from his duffel and sat back against the headboard.

Time to focus.

The problem was that after two paragraphs of a report on the viability of the deep-water port at Nanisivik, his mind returned with the faithfulness of a dog to the bomb-cratered stretch of tarmac slicing through the desert, just beyond a mountain pass. He rubbed his eyes and started the next paragraph, but the words on the page faded away.

He wiped the back of his hand across his mouth, wishing he could spit out the constant grit on his tongue. Even in the G-Wagon with the windows rolled up and AC blasting, sweat dampened his hair under his helmet. In the driver's seat beside him, Corporal Gagnon nattered on about his girlfriend back in Montreal.

"So then she says we've grown apart. Va chier! *I*

thought she was the one. Said she'd wait while I was over here." He snorted. *"Didn't even make it a year. You know—"*

In the sudden silence, Jack asked, "Know what?" He glanced at Gagnon, who sat up straighter, peering intently through the windshield.

Jack tensed. "What is it?"

From the backseat, Grant said, "Is that a kid?"

He jumped at the knock on the door and shoved the scattered papers back into the folder. The door was so light it felt hollow as he opened it. A man waited on the other side wearing a Ranger uniform. He was young and what Jack's mother would call "strapping." Jack cleared his throat.

"Sergeant Carsen?"

The man nodded and saluted.

Jack returned the salute and shook Carsen's hand. "Come in." Jack stepped aside and closed the door. "So…"

Carsen shifted from foot to foot. "Yes, sir?" His voice was low.

"You're the leader of the Arctic Bay Ranger…group?" That much he knew, but he had nothing else to say. He felt like a kid who hadn't done his homework. He supposed that's exactly what he was, which was pathetic given he was thirty-six.

"Yes. The Arctic Bay Patrol."

"Right, patrol." Jack waved a hand. "That's what

I meant. Well, excellent. Uh…" Jack's mind was still blank. Carsen waited, his red baseball cap shadowing his stubbled face. He was just about the same height as Jack, around six feet, yet his quiet presence seemed to fill the room. "And how many people are in your patrol?"

"Twenty-nine."

"Excellent," Jack repeated. *Jesus, I should know this.* "Should we eat? Oh, speaking of which, I brought some chocolate bars if you want any." He opened his duffel and rooted around. "I heard how expensive everything is up here. There are a few Twix, and Crispy Crunch, and let's see…" He glanced back to find Carsen watching impassively. "Do you have a favorite?"

After a few moments, Carsen asked, "Have a Coffee Crisp?"

Jack fished for a yellow wrapper and handed it over. "Here you go."

Carsen didn't meet his gaze. "Thank you." He slipped the bar into the front pocket of his hoodie and cleared his throat. "Uh, dinner should be on now, sir."

The teenagers in the dining room were gone, replaced by two tables of turtlenecked people having a spirited conversation in German. Jack nodded to them, relieved that Carsen chose the table farthest away from the tourists, although the small dining room didn't offer much escape. A teenaged girl appeared, smiling widely.

"Hi, Mr. Carsen. Can I get you a drink?"

Carsen smiled back. "A ginger ale. Thanks, Sedna."

"I'll have a ginger ale too," Jack said.

Sedna nodded. "Tonight there are fish and chips, or caribou meatballs."

Jack didn't have to think about it. "I'll try the caribou."

"Fish and chips," Carsen said.

She hurried back with their ginger ales, placing the cans on the table along with glasses half full of ice and straws in paper wrappers.

When she was gone, Jack asked, "Is she one of your students?"

"Yes." Carsen removed his cap and ran a hand through his short, glossy brownish-black hair.

Jack peeled the paper off his straw and studied Carsen surreptitiously. His nose was thin and lips full. Most strikingly his eyes were a pale steel gray. Carsen dropped his straw into his glass and poured in part of his can. The pop bubbled up to the rim of the glass before evaporating.

"Did you grow up here?"

Carsen blinked. "Don't you have a file on me?"

"Yes, but…I'd still like to hear it from you." Aside from the fact that he hadn't done his prep, Jack realized he also hadn't made small talk in a long time.

Carsen spoke with measured tones. "I was born and raised here. I went to university in Edmonton."

"And you actually came *back*?" Jack joked lamely. "You must really love the cold."

For a long moment, Carsen stared before dropping his gaze to the Formica tabletop. "I suppose I do." He traced the line of a faint crack with his fingertip.

Jack cleared his throat. "What do you teach?"

"English, history and geography. I arranged to have the rest of the week off for your visit, but there was a test today I couldn't reschedule."

"No problem. It was great to meet Ronald. I look forward to meeting the rest of your patrol as well."

"Donald."

"Right. Of course." Christ, he couldn't remember shit these days. He hadn't even brought his dog tags although he was technically in the field. Well, at least with so few people around if he bought it on the tundra he'd be easy to identify.

The silence drew out, and Jack played with his straw. He wished he was back in Ottawa eating a frozen dinner in front of the TV where he couldn't disappoint anyone but himself. He was relieved to spot Sedna approaching with plates. "Here's the food."

Jack's meatballs came with fries and coleslaw, and he dug in with gusto. If he was eating, he couldn't squeeze his foot into his mouth as well. After a minute he said, "This caribou is delicious." He took another bite of the lean, finely textured meat. "It reminds me of venison."

"Yes. There's a similarity."

"What kind of fish is that?" Jack asked. The Germans had gotten their meals as well, and the dining room was silent but for the scrape of cutlery on plates and muffled chewing.

"Turbot. It's also known as Greenland halibut."

"I guess you catch it around here?" *What an incisive observation.* He scooped up some coleslaw.

"Yes."

"So what's up with the booze restriction? You can't drink at all here?"

"Only for special events."

"Oh." Jack waited for Carsen to say more. When he didn't, Jack prompted, "So how does it work?"

"You can apply for a permit, and it has to be approved by the alcohol education committee. It doesn't happen often. Of course there are bootleggers, though. If you'd brought Jack Daniels instead of chocolate you could have turned a nice profit."

Jack smirked. "I bet. Isn't it punishment enough to live up here without having to be sober the entire time?"

Sitting up straighter, Carsen didn't smile. "Most of us don't consider it a punishment."

"No, no, of course not. I just meant…" *What?* "I was just kidding," he finished lamely. Jesus, it almost felt like he was on a bad date. Not that he'd been on a date of any variety in God knew how long. Silence stretched out, and Jack wracked his so-called brain for something to say that wasn't insulting. "Are you married?"

Carsen's expression remained flat as he studied his plate. "No. You?"

"No." Jack dragged a fry through a splotch of ketchup. "Must be hard dating here with so few people. If you don't find the right person…" *Not that I've had better luck with a bigger population pool.* Grant's face flickered in his mind, and Jack shoved it away. He tried to think of some other questions to ask. "Do your parents live here too?"

"My mother. She was born and raised here. My father's a miner from Alberta. Moved there from Scotland to work in the oil sands. He came up here to Nanisivik for a few seasons."

Jack waited for him to say more, but Carsen cut off another piece of breaded fish and chewed slowly. Jack finished his meatballs and grabbed a paper napkin from the dispenser on the table. The Germans were chattering again.

"Do you get many tourists here?"

"Some. More in summer." Carsen finished his last fry. "What time do you want to start in the morning?"

Great question. It would help if I knew what the hell we're doing. "Whatever time you think is best.

Breakfast's at zero-seven-hundred. Unless you want to start earlier?"

"No. Have breakfast first."

"Refresh my memory—where are we going tomorrow?"

Carsen regarded Jack evenly. "Why are you here?"

Another fine question. "They didn't tell you?"

"No. They told me to take you out on patrol and to the mine. Show you around the area, and show you what Rangers do." He wiped his mouth with his napkin and folded it with a neat crease. "Did they tell *you?*"

Jack smiled tightly, fidgeting at the way Carsen seemed to see right through him. "Of course." He glanced at the Germans and lowered his voice. "They're considering a permanent training base in the area." That much he did know at least. "Our soldiers are trained for the desert, but not the Arctic. We have to plan for the future."

Carsen's smooth brow furrowed. "Permanent? But the government backed out of the naval base. We were glad of it."

"Why's that?"

"It wasn't going to do anything for our community. They wouldn't allow cruise ships to use the port. No money coming into Arctic Bay, and probably a negative impact on hunting and the environment. We were relieved when they backed off."

"Look, honestly? This whole trip is a waste of time. As much is going to come from this as it did from the grand plans for a naval base at the old mine. I'll make a report, and a bunch of committees in Ottawa will examine it, and in the end they won't have the budget for it anyway. So it doesn't really matter."

After a long moment, Carsen said, "Fair enough." He finished his ginger ale with a loud slurp through his straw. "I'll meet you outside at seven-thirty tomorrow. We're going on patrol. Unless you want to just skip it."

He was sorely tempted. "No, of course not. We have to go through the motions." He grimaced. "It's a pain."

"Do you know how to dress for patrol?"

"Warmly, I imagine."

Carsen's smile was sharp. "Indeed. We'll be out for two nights. I have all the equipment. Wear layers."

"Arctic camping trip, huh?" *Terrific.* "Layers it is."

Carsen stood up and pushed in his chair. "I assume Ottawa's paying for dinner." He raised his hand to his forehead in a salute.

"Yes, of course." Jack moved to stand, but Carsen was already striding from the dining room. Jack watched him go with a sigh. This would be a fun few days of awkward silences and stilted conversation.

Sedna returned, and Jack gave her a twenty dollar tip and told her to charge the meal to his hotel bill. She beamed, and he felt a little better as he returned to his room. Still, he cringed as he replayed dinner with Sergeant Carsen over and over in his mind as he sat on his bed and tried to finally read the briefing package. *Way to make a great first impression.*

"What do I care what this guy thinks of me?" He sighed, realizing Neville wasn't there to listen to him with head cocked, as if everything Jack said was endlessly fascinating. He supposed it was in a pug's mind. "Okay. Time to focus. And stop talking to myself."

He scanned the file on Carsen. *Kinguyakkii Carsen. Thirty-three years old. Unmarried. One of the youngest Ranger sergeants in the service. Teacher.* There wasn't much there. Jack flipped through the papers, but that was all the info he had on Carsen. He went back to the report on the navy's aborted plans for a base at Nanisivik, yet every few minutes he eyed Carsen's file as if he expected new words to have appeared.

When he switched off the light to rack out, he found himself staring at the ceiling, listening to the rumble of German vibrating through the thin walls. He replayed his entire encounter with Carsen once again through his mind, thinking of everything he should have said and done differently. He was a captain for fuck's sake. This assignment might be a waste of time, but it was no excuse to show up unprepared.

He'd been phoning it in for months at his desk in Ottawa, and it was time to get his shit together. He may not want to be here on this Godforsaken hunk of rock and ice, but he would do his job, and do it well. He owed Etienne that much. Hell, he owed himself that much, not to mention the people of Arctic Bay.

Tomorrow he'd make nice with Carsen and try to un-fuck the lousy impression he'd undoubtedly made. He just needed to get through the next few days with a minimum of stress and bullshit.

And then what? Back to Ottawa and pushing paper?

Sergeant Carsen's unflinching gray gaze filled his mind again, refusing to leave. But as Jack drifted off, memories of a sun-soaked desert road and too-quiet morning stayed away, and that was something.

Chapter Two

A WASTE OF TIME.

Captain Turner sure had that right. As Kin packed up the *komatik* in the darkness just after seven a.m., he had half a mind to call the whole thing off. What was the point of dragging some uselessly handsome southerner out on patrol when neither of them wanted to be there? He could make up some excuse. Turner would probably be just as glad for it.

"Morning." Walter Pimniq lifted a hand in greeting as he came out of his house next door. He gazed up at the void of a sky. "More snow coming soon, I think. Are you going to show the captain how to build an igloo? Southerners like that." He sipped steaming coffee from an insulated plastic cup. He wasn't wearing a hat, and his graying black hair was tousled.

"Maybe." Kin fastened a tarp over the tightly packed komatik, making sure the load of gasoline cans, a tent, stove and other supplies were fastened securely. A Canadian flag stood proudly at the front of the sled, flapping in the wind.

"How's your new snow machine?"

Kin grinned as he patted the snowmobile's side. "Fast."

"I bet." Walter sipped his coffee. "Lisa's watching your classes?"

"Uh-huh." The Arctic Bay grapevine operated with a ruthless efficiency, and Kin knew Walter was well aware Lisa Innugati was subbing for his classes the rest of the week. She wasn't officially a teacher, but she was good with the kids and would make sure they did the assignments Kin left. At least he'd only had to take two days off work for this farce of an army visit.

Walter's smile was sly. "I bet she was happy to do it."

"Yes. She likes the kids."

"And you."

Kin resisted the urge to sigh, instead smiling easily. "She's a good friend, but it didn't work out between us."

"But you were just kids then. You still hung up on that girl back west?"

"Afraid so."

His imaginary university girlfriend had *really* broken his heart. Kin knew everyone wondered why he didn't marry or even date. Sometimes he thought they must know the truth about him, but it didn't seem to cross anyone's mind. That was the Arctic for you.

He'd never met another gay person in Nunavut, although he knew he couldn't be the only one. But without roads between communities, it's not as if they could meet up. Even the Nunavut capital only had a population of seven thousand people.

Walter kicked his boot in the fresh snow that had fallen overnight and blanketed the community. "That captain say why he's here?"

This was the question on everyone's minds, of course. Kin shrugged and double checked the hitch that attached the komatik to the back of his snowmobile. "Just a Ranger inspection. No big deal."

"Routine, huh?" Walter didn't seem convinced.

Kin climbed onto the snowmobile. "Yep."

"Well, do us proud. You always do."

He smiled. "Thanks, Walter."

He'd turned off the lights and made sure the door was locked—a habit he'd picked up in Edmonton. Kin didn't have anything of real value in the house, which was little more than a bedroom, bathroom and common area with kitchen on one end. His books meant the most to him, and it wasn't as though anyone would want those. He didn't have any video games or moonshine, so he was safe.

Lights flickered on through Arctic Bay as Kin drove over to the hotel. It was getting near the end of

October, with snowmobiles becoming the main mode of transportation. He was early, so he cut the engine when he reached the Siqiniq. As the sky lightened almost imperceptibly, Kin watched his breath clouding the air and listened to Turner's voice in his head.

A waste of time. Doesn't matter.

He sighed as his skin prickled and flushed. The worst part wasn't that he had to take two days off work right when his students were preparing for their midterm exams, but that he'd actually been *excited.* Proud, even. An army captain coming to Arctic Bay!

He'd been nervous all week, planning the patrol route and fielding suggestions from everyone he came across as to the best places to take Turner to show off their home. Too bad the arrogant ass couldn't care less. Kin had been worried he'd say the wrong thing, but clearly he needn't have bothered giving it any thought at all.

The door to the hotel opened and the captain emerged as if on cue. Kin stood and saluted, and Turner saluted back.

"Good morning. No need to salute. We don't need to stand on ceremony out here."

Doesn't want to waste his time. "All right, Captain Turner."

"And please, call me Jack."

There was no choice but to return the gesture. "Kin."

"Kin. Very good." He waved a hand over his olive green snow pants and parka. He wore thick white boots instead of the combat boots he'd arrived in, and his rifle was strapped over his shoulder. "I wore layers. Are you sure I don't need to bring anything else?"

"Yes. I'll put your rifle on the sled with mine." Kin reached a hand out for it, even though the thing would likely be useless if the temperature dipped too low.

Turner—*Jack*—passed him the weapon. "Is that thing going to hold together?" He nodded to the komatik.

No. That's why I'm bringing it. "There's more give this way." He pointed to where the cross boards were lashed to the sled with rope. "Nail it together and it'll disintegrate in a few miles bumping along on this terrain."

"Ah. That makes sense."

I know, Kin thought.

"The town's quiet in the morning. I guess it never gets too noisy, huh?"

"Hamlet."

Jack frowned. "Sorry?"

"It's not a town. We have hamlets in Nunavut." Kin was being pedantic, but couldn't help himself.

"Oh." Jack gazed around. "It snowed, huh?" A moment later he shook his head with a smile. "Maybe you should call me Captain Obvious."

He had a nice smile. His lips were wide and red, and a little thin, which matched his square jaw. He was freshly shaved, and he pulled a woolen toque over his dark blond hair.

"So, uh…what are your pants made of?" Jack asked.

Kin realized he was staring and jerked his gaze away. "Caribou." The fur pants were tucked into his shin-high boots, and his heavy black parka reached mid-thigh. It was only about minus ten, and he didn't really need to wear his full winter gear. But you never knew how the weather could turn out on the tundra.

"Looks cozy."

Kin held up his furry gloves. "Grizzly bear." He reached into his backpack, which was stored on the back of the snowmobile. He passed Jack a steel bottle of water. "Tuck it into a pocket inside your parka. Keep it close to your body so it won't freeze."

Jack did as he was told, and next Kin passed over a woolen neck warmer that could be pulled up over the mouth and nose, and a large pair of clear goggles. "I have polarized lenses for when the sun's up. Clear's best for the dark." He put on his own goggles before pulling up his fur-lined hood over his red toque. He straddled the snowmobile and started the engine. "We should get going."

"No helmets?" Jack's voice was muffled under the neck warmer.

Kin hesitated. "I could get some. But hardly anyone wears helmets up here. I know we should, but…" He shrugged.

"Nah, it's fine. What time does the sun come up?" Jack asked as he climbed on behind Kin.

"About nine."

"Will you be able to see where we're going before then?"

Kin bristled. "I know this land."

"Of course. I didn't—"

"You'd better hold on." Kin pulled his neck warmer up over his nose. Jack may think this was pointless, but Kin would still show him that the Rangers knew what they were doing.

He kept the engine low through town, but soon they sped into the morning twilight. Jack's arms were solid around him, and even through all their layers, it was strangely intimate and awkward. Kin had ridden with people plenty of times before, but there was something about Jack Turner that put him off balance.

Even with only seven hours of sunlight, it was going to be a long day.

As THE SUN peeked out from a bank of gray clouds a couple hours later, Kin stopped the snowmobile and climbed off, letting his goggles hang around his neck.

Jack pulled off his goggles and gazed around. "It's very…"

Kin braced.

"Stark. Lunar, almost. Like the moon with snow. You can see for miles."

He relaxed a little. It was true enough. They were on a wide plateau of the Borden Peninsula with fresh snow covering the arid land, and even though the air nipped his lungs, Kin breathed deeply. As much as he hated missing work when his students needed him, it was a fine day to be out on the tundra. He pulled his rifle from the sled and handed it to Jack. "Take this."

"Whoa." Jack hefted the rifle and ran a gloved hand along the barrel. "An Enfield, right? Three-oh-three caliber bolt action?"

Kin nodded.

"I thought the PM was replacing these relics? These are World War II rifles. We haven't used these since the Korean War at the latest."

With a shrug, Kin pulled out a small metal box from the sled. "The government's been saying that for years. It keeps getting pushed back. I don't mind, though. Enfields still have a big advantage over your fancy new rifles."

Jack raised an eyebrow. "And that is…?"

"The mechanism doesn't freeze. Gets down to forty, fifty below in the winter. Colder. I'd rather have a rifle I know works, even if it's old."

Peering around, Jack said, "Can't imagine there's much call for using it."

"Never know who you might find out here." Kin pulled off his right glove to open the fiddly latch on the box holding his compass.

"Why, are the Russians coming?" Jack smiled.

"No. But the polar bears are already here."

Jack's eyes widened and he jerked his head around.

Kin chuckled despite himself. "Not right this second. They tend to stay by the coast, but sometimes they travel inland. We have to be vigilant."

For a moment, Jack still squinted at the horizon, turning in a slow circle before his shoulders lowered. "That's your motto, right? The Rangers?"

"Yes. *Vigilans*. The watchers." Kin slipped his hand back into his glove before his fingers got numb, but left the compass in the box for the moment. "What do you know about us? The Rangers, I mean?"

Jack lowered the butt of the rifle to his boot. "You're part of the CF Reserve, and this is 1 CRPG, which encompasses Nunavut, the Yukon, Northwest Territories, and Atlin, in the far north of British Columbia."

Kin almost asked him to spell the acronyms out for the rest of the class—Canadian Forces; Canadian Ranger Patrol Group—before remembering his students weren't there. *Maybe I do need a few days off.*

Jack went on. "More than eighty percent of Rangers in 1 CRPG are Inuit and speak Inuktitut as your first language. Some speak Dene, or other Inuit languages. You're CF's eyes and ears in the Arctic. You participate in northern training operations, check the North Warning System radar sites, report suspicious and unusual activities, assist in search and rescue, and collect local data of military significance."

Captain Turner had apparently done his homework last night. Or at least spent a few minutes Googling. "Yes. But what do you actually *know* about us?"

"I…" He sighed. "Look, I don't know much. But since I'm here, I'd like to learn. I'm all ears." He glanced around. "And eyes. Is there a trick for spotting polar bears, by the way?"

So now Jack wanted to learn? That was progress, Kin supposed. "Not really. Just watch for movement. And claws. Not to mention teeth."

"I feel like Luke Skywalker on Hoth."

Surprised, Kin laughed. "Just before the snow monster drags him into his lair?"

"Exactly. You'll rescue me, right? Are there any tauntauns for us to sleep inside?"

"Afraid not. I'll just have to keep you warm myself." As the words left his mouth, Kin's face flushed. Carter was going to think he was flirting if he wasn't careful. "That was my favorite movie growing up."

Jack smiled. "Me too. I know it off by heart. All

three of the originals."

Kin discovered that Jack's eyes crinkled in the corners when he smiled for real and wasn't only going through the motions of being polite. "New trilogy doesn't count."

"Nope. Also, Han shot first."

Well, at least they had *Star Wars* in common. "That he did."

"Nice snowmobile, by the way."

"Shouldn't you call it an LOSV?"

Jack smirked. "Ah yes, the official military term. I've been dealing with deserts my whole career. What is it again? Light over-snow vehicle? Well, I guess I can call it that if I want to come across as even more of a dick. Which I don't, for the record. I have a bad habit of saying exactly the wrong thing."

Kin blinked, surprised again. He wasn't sure how to respond. "Apology accepted." He removed the black metal device from the box.

Jack's gaze zeroed in on what Kin was holding. "Is that an astrocompass?"

"It is." Kin found himself smiling, a little shocked that Jack knew it by sight. He leveled it on a flat space on the back of the sled and pointed it north. It was similar in shape to a small microscope, but with a base plate marked with compass points and a round drum and dials above. "You've used one before?"

Jack kneeled by the sled, one hand propping the

rifle beside him in the snow. His lips parted, and his eyes were bright as he examined the compass. "Not for years. As a cadet I spent some time at Valcatraz." He glanced up. "CFB Valcartier, near Quebec City. One of the instructors showed us how to use this." He pointed. "That's the equatorial drum, right? With the sights on top? You adjust it according to latitude and time of day, and angle of the sun or whatever star you're using?"

Kin found himself smiling. "That's right." He grabbed the table he'd printed out with the local hour angle for the sun and other stars for the next few days. "I have GPS with me, but it can be unreliable up here, and this will never run out of juice or freeze up." He shrugged. "And this is just fun to use. For me, anyway."

"Me too." Jack grinned and examined his watch. "And this close to the North Pole, magnetic compasses go wonky." He peered at the astrocompass again like a kid with a new toy. "But this will show us true north."

"You want to try it?"

"Can I?"

Nodding, Kin took the rifle and passed Jack the printout. "I've never met anyone who was interested in this stuff. Are you into astronomy?"

Jack smiled again, and little sexy wrinkles fanned out from his eyes. "Since I was a little kid. You?"

Kin's belly was fluttering like a bird was trapped

inside. *He's not sexy. Stop thinking that. So what if he likes Han Solo and astronomy? And yes, he apologized, but...* He nodded. "Before my father left, he used to show me all the stars." Why had he said that? He barely talked about his father with anyone, let alone a stranger. He stood and pulled a thermos from the pack and took a swig before offering it to Jack. "Warm cider? We'll melt ice for water when we stop for the night."

"Sure, thanks." Jack had a few sips, his throat working as he swallowed. "Okay, I think I have the settings right."

"If the sun is in the sights, then the compass will show true north." Kin crouched next to Jack. "There we go."

"Are we at the right coordinates?" Jack leaned over to examine the side of the compass, and his breath fanned Kin's cheek.

Kin nodded, trying to ignore the shiver that shot down his spine. "I just like to double check. Actually I just like to use the astrocompass."

"Where are we headed?"

"We're skirting around the south end of the national park. Sirmilik, it's called. Then we'll head west on the peninsula in a couple of days, back toward the coast. See what we see." He and Jack were shoulder to shoulder at the end of the sled, somehow crouching very close to each other. Kin shot to his feet. "Hungry?" He unzipped a plastic bag of partially frozen raw seal and handed it over.

With a furrow between his brows, Jack took the bag. "Is it liver?"

"Seal." Kin swallowed a chunk of the smooth, beet-red meat. It was a little thicker when it was frozen, but still went down easily.

"Raw?" Jack pulled off his glove and picked up a piece. He chewed it thoughtfully. "Huh. It's fishy, but…reminds me of game meat as well."

"A lot of southerners balk at eating seal."

Jack shrugged. "When in Rome. Why do you eat it raw?"

"Out here it's better. My grandfather always said it cooks in the stomach. Gives you more energy."

Jack swallowed another piece and passed back the bag. "The aftertaste is like…"

"Iron," Kin suggested, taking another piece for himself. He chewed a few times before it slipped down his throat. "I have a few granola and protein bars too."

"Sure. I wouldn't mind a granola chaser. Hey, what do vegetarians eat up here if they don't do fish?"

Kin smiled wryly. "Any vegetarians here are from down south."

"Really? Huh. I guess it makes sense. Not a lot of tofu on the tundra."

With a chuckle, Kin shook his head. "Not much. What we'd call a vegetarian is a word that means 'bad hunter.'"

"Ah. Good thing I didn't ask for the vegetarian option at dinner last night." He winced. "Or vegan, God forbid."

Kin laughed. "No, the Arctic isn't the place for someone who wants to avoid animal products."

"Survival of the fittest, right? Speaking of which, do you see many polar bears?"

Kin pondered it. "I see enough. Had a close call once when I was camping on patrol. Woke up in the night to find a polar bear pawing at my buddy Michael. Good thing he still had his boots on after getting up to piss. Bear shredded half our tent, but we managed to get a shot off and I guess it decided we were too much hassle."

"Arctic insurgents."

Kin smiled. "Something like that. At least with a polar bear you know what you're going to get. They don't plant bombs."

Jack's gaze went distant, and he took off his gloves to peel the wrapper on a granola bar. "That's something at least."

A question about what it was like in Afghanistan circled Kin's mind, but he popped another piece of seal into his mouth before he asked. The silence was surprisingly easy. The day wasn't turning out so bad after all.

After a minute, Jack asked, "You're young to be elected a Ranger sergeant, aren't you?"

KEIRA ANDREWS

He shrugged. "Yes. When the old sergeant died, somehow the patrol started looking to me. Maybe because I'm a teacher. I don't know."

"You must be well respected in the community."

Kin's stomach twisted with a familiar flood of acid. "I suppose." But the people of Arctic Bay didn't truly know him. If they did... He took a deep breath, his chest tightening. "I've always wanted to be a Ranger."

"Must be kind of fun. You don't have to worry about anything actually happening out here."

While he knew it was true that the Arctic was a far cry from Afghanistan, Kin still bristled at Jack's dismissive tone. "We may not be trained for combat, but if something ever happens you'll need us. You southerners wouldn't last a day out here without our help." He grabbed the rifle and repacked the sled. He welcomed the irritation. Irritation was good. Irritation was safe. "We need to get moving."

Jack held up his hands. "Look, I'm—"

But Kin turned the engine on, and the roar filled the air. It was too loud to talk once they started off across the tundra again, and that was probably a good thing. This was official business, and it wasn't as if he and Captain Jack Turner needed to be friends. Kin certainly didn't need to be finding the man *sexy*. No, what he needed was to do his job. Nothing less, and definitely nothing more.

BY FOUR O'CLOCK the sun was below the horizon, and Kin pounded in the last tent peg.

"Those pegs must be titanium to get through the permafrost," Jack said. He was on predator watch, and scanned the horizon with Kin's binoculars.

"Just about." Kin was flushed beneath all his layers, and he hurried to raise the poles and get the tent up. "My hammer shattered once. It was pretty cold that day."

"What's your definition of 'pretty cold'?"

He pondered it. "Once we get below minus forty, that's pretty cold. This isn't bad."

"Feels like it's getting a little colder." Jack glanced at his watch. "Five degrees Fahrenheit. About minus fifteen."

"Yeah, about that. Why is your watch in Fahrenheit?" Kin fastened the guylines on the tent in case the wind blew up. The clouds had partly dissipated, and stars twinkled into view as the light faded.

"It was a gift from an American. She was a staff sergeant in Kabul. Gave it to me before she went home to Knoxville."

Ah. Probably a girlfriend. Kin felt strangely disappointed, although he had no reason to care if Jack was straight. He concentrated on transferring their equipment inside. First he spread out a few hides. He lit a lantern and hung it from a hook on the apex of the tent.

"How are we going to sleep out here?" Jack called. "Jesus, how do you do it in the dead of winter?"

"We just do."

In the tent, Kin fired up the Coleman stove. The green metal rectangle had two burners, and he'd made sure the little red fuel tank attached to the side was full before leaving. They had extra stove fuel packed away, but it could be a pain to refill it when you needed to get warm as soon as possible. "You can come in now. Leave your boots just inside the door."

He took off his own boots and put on his caribou booties over his thick thermal socks as Jack crawled inside, placing the rifle carefully by the door. Kin passed Jack a spare pair of slippers. "Put these on. Toes get frostbitten easily."

Jack gazed around. "This is nice. No igloo?"

Kin smiled. "I could build one, but the tent is easier. It depends on the weather and snow conditions. I try to build a few every winter so I don't forget how. Some of the young people these days aren't learning the survival skills we all used to have. But my grandfather made sure I knew."

"Is it safe to have a stove in here?"

"The tent's inside layer is flame resistant polyester. Arctic grade and breathable so our breath won't condense and frost inside." The two-man tent was generously sized, and there was enough room to sit up comfortably with a few feet of headroom. Kin made sure the outer and inner doors were zipped tightly. "The outer shell is wind resistant. If the wind gets bad I have a saw to make a break wind."

"Out of snow?"

He nodded. "Like an igloo without a roof."

"God, it feels good to get warm again. Makes a big difference just being in here." Jack pulled off his gloves and rubbed his hands, holding them near the stove as it heated up. "What's for dinner?"

"I'll heat up some bannock and tea. I brought dried caribou as well as the seal." He put a few chunks of ice in a pot to boil, and warmed the round bannock on a pan on the other burner. Soon they tore off chunks and sipped their tea.

Jack groaned. "Delicious. I haven't had bannock in years. It's like a big biscuit."

Kin was ridiculously pleased by the praise—and flushed by the sound Jack had made. *Stop. Don't even think about it. This is just business. He's an arrogant pain in the ass, remember?*

"Oh, you've got…" Jack pointed.

Kin wiped crumbs from the corner of his mouth. "Did I get it?"

Jack's gaze flicked from Kin's mouth to his eyes and back again. "Uh-huh."

They sat cross-legged by the stove on bear and caribou hides. The tent was warm enough now, and their parkas were piled by the door. They were both in their uniforms, and Kin brushed crumbs from his red sweatshirt. He had some of the dried caribou and rooted around in the food box. "Do you like peaches?"

Jack's mouth was full, but he nodded.

Kin opened the can and sat it in the pan. Before long, the peach juice simmered, and he passed Jack a fork.

"Oh my God." Jack ate a peach with his eyes closed. "Canned peaches have never tasted this good."

"In the Arctic everything tastes good. Especially if it's warm." Kin speared a wedge with his fork and savored the soft fruit. The sweet juice dripped down his chin, and he swiped at it before sucking his finger. When he glanced up to offer the can, Jack was staring at him, red in his cheeks and the shine of peach juice on his lips.

Kin's belly flip-flopped like a fish in the bottom of a boat. He tore his gaze back to the can in his hand and said the first thing that came into his mind that didn't involve wanting to lick the juice from Jack's mouth. "This is my grandfather's specialty. He had to count them out for me and my brother or we'd fight over who got more."

As soon as the words were out, the buzz flowing through him vanished as memories spun through his mind. *Snatching a peach from his little brother's bowl, and Maguyuk's howl of outrage filling the igloo.*

"I bet." Jack smiled. "Was your grandfather a Ranger?"

Kin shoved the memories away. "He was. He's retired now. Says he's too old to be out here, but he still hunts and fishes as much as he ever did."

"How about your brother? Is he still in Arctic Bay?"

Kin's throat felt like sandpaper. "No." He gulped his cooling tea.

"Where did he move to?" Jack scooped up another peach wedge.

"He's dead."

Jack's fork hovered by his mouth, and he lowered it without eating the fruit. "I'm sorry."

Kin drank more tea. "Thanks." He braced for the inevitable questions.

"Say, polar bears don't like peaches, do they?"

His breath rushed out, and Kin managed a grateful smile. "Nah. They're partial to pineapple."

"I thought as much. Bet they like that tropical fruit cocktail." Jack passed back the can.

"Yeah." He swallowed another peach. "I'd better do a scan."

"Can I come along?"

Kin frowned. "Are you sure you want to go back out there?"

"When in Rome, right? Unless I'll be in your way."

"You won't be in my way."

As Kin turned off the stove and geared up, he tried to make sense of it all. Most people he met fit into neat little boxes in his mind, but Captain Jack Turner seemed determined to messily squeeze into the nooks and crannies.

Chapter Three

JESUS CHRIST IT was cold.

With fingers stiff in his gloves, Jack flicked on his little flashlight under his sleeping bag. It was only zero-four-hundred, but it had been dark for so many hours it felt as though the night would never end. It must have clouded over, since there was no light from the moon making its way through the tent walls. He shuddered to think of what it was like in the winter when the sun barely rose at all.

Carefully, he pointed the flashlight around the tent, aiming it high to avoid waking Kin, who slept peacefully a few feet away. The red of Kin's toque peeked out from his sleeping bag, and Jack could see his closed eyes and his nose. He was breathing deeply and evenly.

The odds of turning on the stove without waking him were nil, so Jack stayed put, shivering in his sleeping bag. Kin didn't seem bothered by the cold at all, but Jack's teeth chattered. He wanted to wrap himself in one of the pelts beneath them, but the idea of moving out of his bag was not appealing.

He should have turned off the flashlight since he was wasting the battery, but he found himself watching Kin sleep. He'd shared tents with dozens of men over the years, but none had intrigued him like Kin Carsen did. *Not even Grant.* He winced at the familiar sting of guilt twisting in his gut.

His scars flared to life, and he scrabbled at the back of his neck and shoulder, dropping the flashlight with a thud, the beam of light spinning around the tent. It was as if his flesh was burning again, and it prickled unbearably. He yanked off his gloves to scratch properly, squirming in the tight sleeping bag.

"Jack?" Kin murmured.

"I'm fine," he gritted out. "Go back to sleep."

Kin's tone was sharp, all drowsiness vanished. "What is it?"

The light shone in his face, and Jack squeezed his eyes shut and burrowed into his bag. "I said it's nothing. Leave me the hell alone." He dug his blunt nails into his skin even though he knew it would pass faster if he left the scars untouched. The doctors said the itching was all in his head, but it was hard to believe when he trembled with hot prickles. At least he didn't feel as cold.

"I'm only trying to help."

"Then *don't.* I don't need your help."

"Well, excuse the fuck out of me. *Sir*."

The flashlight snapped off, and when Jack opened his eyes the tent was black again. *Fuck. Fuck, fuck, fuck.* He breathed heavily through his nose, forcing himself to stop scratching. "I'm sorry. It's not you, okay? It's a hundred percent me. I'm a bag of shit lately."

There was silence for a long moment. Then, "Is that the official diagnosis?"

Jack barked out a laugh, some of the tension leeching from his body. He felt around for his gloves but couldn't find them, so he curled his hands against his chest in the sleeping bag. "It should be. Sorry for being a drama queen. You're more patient than I would be stuck with an FNG."

"You'll have to enlighten me."

"Fucking new guy."

Kin laughed softly, and Jack wished he could see the little dimples that creased his cheeks. He tried to think of something else he could say to make him laugh. "I wouldn't blame you if your GAFF was pretty low right now."

"Okay, I'll bite."

"Give a fuck factor."

Kin laughed again, and despite the cold Jack felt a bloom of warmth in his chest.

"Do you have an army to English dictionary? My kids would love these."

"No, but someone should write one."

"Maybe that should be your next assignment."

"Maybe."

Jack breathed easily again. There was something nice about talking in the dark in their sleeping bags. Reminded him of when he was a kid staying over at Jimmy Leclerc's house, talking until all hours of the night on the old shag carpet in the basement. And just like he had with Jimmy, Jack inched closer to Kin, shifting himself as quietly as possible.

He didn't know why he had that urge, since he was a grown man now and he didn't have the excuse of being afraid of the dark, or the rumbles and clangs from the Leclercs' furnace. Outside the tent there was only the steady whisper of wind. But he still felt drawn to Kin, and the low sound of his exhalations.

"What's it like during the midnight sun? When there's daylight twenty four hours?"

"It's…lively. The restaurant at the hotel is open day and night since there's always someone awake. I try to keep normal hours, but it's hard. There's a lot more noise, and people out and about. We pretty much hibernate in the winter and make up for it in the summer."

"Must be strange. I guess you get used to it."

"Yeah. It's just the way it is. Everyone has black-out curtains. But there's always a party going on somewhere. Once—"

Jack waited a few heartbeats. "Once what?"

"My brother snuck off and went fishing with his

buddies in the middle of the night. They 'borrowed' a boat, and of course they got caught since there they were in the middle of the bay, clear as day. Even in the winter, there's always someone watching. Hard to keep secrets in Arctic Bay."

"Have you tried?"

Kin was silent for a moment. "Everyone has something to hide."

It was all Jack could do not to ask. But he had his own secrets, and it was best to keep it all locked away, no matter how safe it felt cocooned in the dark with Kin. Anything Jack said tonight could haunt him in the dawn.

"That's why I like coming out here. There's only the land, and it keeps all its secrets."

"How about the polar bears?"

Kin chuckled. "They're the worst gossips. Never tell a polar bear something you don't want the whole world to know."

"I'll keep that in mind next time I'm shooting the breeze with one." Jack flexed his fingers, rubbing his bare hands together. "Christ it's cold. I dropped my gloves."

Kin's tone was sharper. "You did?"

Material rustled and Jack expected the flashlight to come on. But his heart skipped a beat as Kin spoke.

"Give me your hands." Kin's voice was closer.

Jack's mouth went dry, and he heard his heartbeat thumping in his ears like when he wore earplugs on planes. He shimmied his arms out of the sleeping bag and fumbled for Kin. When their fingers brushed together, he had to bite back a gasp at the flare of desire in his belly.

Smoothly, Kin took Jack's hands between his and rubbed. He'd taken off his own gloves, and he massaged Jack's fingers. God, it felt good. Kin's hands were slightly callused—more so than Jack would expect from a teacher. Granted he was also a Ranger, but a Saturday soldier didn't usually get his hands that dirty.

"Why didn't you say anything? Frostbite can happen really easily out here. You have to be careful. Your fingers are way too cold."

Jack opened his mouth to give some kind of excuse, but any words were lost in a strangled gurgle when his index finger was enveloped by wet heat. Kin sucked, and his tongue swirled around, rough and slick at the same time. Jack was glad he wasn't standing, since so much blood rushed to his cock he likely would have gotten lightheaded.

A *pop* echoed in the tent as Kin released that finger, sounding positively obscene. Jack was grateful for the pitch darkness as he opened his mouth to pant silently.

"Sorry," Kin murmured. "It's the best way to warm up fingers. If you get frostbite we'll have to go back in the morning." He moved to the next one, sucking it down past the second knuckle.

Jack struggled to keep his voice even as his pulse skyrocketed with every swipe of Kin's tongue. "It's fine."

Jesus, it was one of the most erotic things he'd ever felt. Kin clasped Jack's left hand as he methodically sucked the fingers on the right, and Jack had to concentrate on not gripping Kin's palm. He bit his tongue to stifle the moans clawing at his throat. Kin's hot breath skimmed across Jack's skin, and his mouth—Christ, his *mouth*.

What would it feel like on Jack's cock? At the thought, his hips stuttered, his dick swelling and desperate for friction. The urge to squirm closer and hump Kin's leg was almost overwhelming. Had he really been cold a minute ago? Now his whole body was alight, rigid with want.

He dug his teeth into his lower lip. Fuck, the things Kin was doing with his tongue. The torture was exquisite, and his fingers tingled hotly. It could be painful warming up too-cold skin, but all Jack could focus on was Kin's mouth.

Kin moved on to his left hand. Jack's right fingers were wet, and he wanted to lick them and taste the residue of Kin's saliva. But Kin kept hold of both hands, murmuring something around his finger. It was for the best, since if Jack got a hand free he wasn't sure he'd be able to resist diving beneath his layers and jerking himself off, even if Kin heard what he was doing. His cock strained and leaked in his briefs.

Opening his mouth on a silent moan, he imagined Kin's tongue not only on his cock, but all over his body. Licking across his nipples, and down to his belly. On the insides of his thighs, and over his tight balls. Behind them to his hole.

Jack spread his legs as much as he could in his sleeping bag, as if he could will Kin's mouth to his body. To feel that tongue everywhere would be heaven. As Kin sucked Jack's little finger, Jack imagined he was naked with Kin's face buried in his crotch.

Then the heat was gone, and Kin held Jack's hands between both of his again, drying them methodically with some kind of soft fabric.

"Better?"

Was it Jack's imagination, or was Kin a little breathless? He cleared his throat. "Uh-huh."

For a few moments, the only sound was their heavy breathing and the rub of the towel or scarf or whatever it was against Jack's fingers. Then Kin spoke again. "We should find your gloves. Where's the flashlight?"

"I found them," Jack blurted. His flushed face would give him away in a heartbeat.

"How?"

Jack realized Kin still had his hands. "They were here all along in my pocket. I just realized." His voice was unnaturally high. He took a deep breath. "Thank you."

"No problem."

It wasn't so much that Kin was holding Jack's hands now, but that they were holding each other's across the little space still separating them. What would happen if Jack tugged Kin closer? If he pulled Kin on top of him, and found his mouth in the darkness, and rutted up against him, and—

Kin let go. "We should get more sleep. Sun won't be up for hours."

"Right. See you in the morning."

As he listened to Kin's ragged breathing, Jack silently searched for his gloves, hoping he could get his shit together by the time the sun rose.

KIN HAD TO stop thinking about Jack's cock.

He gave himself a mental shake as he drove the snowmobile over a low rise. Jack was pressed up against him, his hands on Kin's waist. Kin squinted against the glare of the sun, noting the rise and fall of the land and veering gently to the left, keeping them on a southerly course on the outskirts of Sirmilik.

Is he cut or uncut? Kin couldn't stop imagining how Jack would feel and taste in his mouth, the shaft thick and heavy on his tongue, stretching his lips and filling him. How he'd feel in Kin's hand, and the sounds Jack would make as he stroked him. Kin's groan rumbled through his chest.

"Okay?" Jack called over the noise of the engine.

Kin nodded. What had he been thinking, sucking Jack's fingers like that? Granted, Jack had genuinely been in danger of frostbite, but Kin had felt like a dog in heat ever since. If the slaps wouldn't have echoed in the tent, he'd have jerked himself off to the fantasy of touching the rest of Jack. Kissing him.

Enough! He had to stop. He was never going to kiss or touch Captain Jack Turner. It wasn't going to happen. He needed to focus on doing his job and not humiliating himself. Apparently he'd been celibate too long, because he was losing it.

"Can we take a break?" Jack shouted.

Kin slowed at the bottom of a hill in a wide valley. When they came to a stop, Jack climbed off, and Kin felt foolishly bereft without the other man pressed against him. What was the matter with him?

The wind was calm, and with the sun beaming down, Kin's hair was damp under his toque. They both kept on their polarized goggles to block the glare. "Are you hungry?" he asked Jack.

"I can always eat."

Kin glanced over at where Jack had gone to piss. His back was turned, and Kin could hear the stream of urine where it hit the snow. He swallowed hard.

"Guess it's not cold enough to freeze in the air,

huh?"

Kin forced a laugh. "No. Has to be about minus forty for that. We're only at minus fifteen."

"Balmy," Jack said.

He listened to Jack zipping up his layers, unable to look away until Jack turned. Kin jerked his head down and picked up the Enfield. "Want to be on predator watch while I make lunch?"

"Sure." Jack took the rifle.

"We can do some target practice if you want."

Jack scoffed, but it was good-natured. "Who says I need target practice?"

"It's different firing an old rifle. Your fancy new weapons do half the work for you."

"Is that so?" Jack's lips twitched. "Sounds like a challenge."

Kin smiled. "You use my rifle and I'll use yours?"

"Deal. What are we hitting?"

He rooted around in the crate where he kept the garbage. "Peach cans at a hundred paces?"

After setting the cans on a rocky ledge, Kin rejoined Jack, who handed him his C7 assault rifle. It was a little lighter than the Enfield, and Kin examined it, getting used to the feel of it. Meanwhile, Jack took off his goggles and lifted the Enfield to his shoulder.

Kin said, "You'll want to—"

The shot rang out, missing both cans by approximately a mile. Kin swallowed his laughter and cleared his throat. "There's probably more kick than you're used to."

Jack huffed. "No, I just got distracted because you started talking."

"Ah, that must have been it." Kin rolled his tongue in his cheek. He pointed to the targets and made a zipping motion across his mouth. He took off his goggles and held up a hand to block the sun.

With a deep breath, Jack lifted the rifle and squinted down the barrel. He squeezed off another shot, and this one at least pinged off the rocks beneath the cans. He cursed under his breath. "Okay. Apparently I need some pointers after all."

"Can I speak now?" Kin couldn't help but smile.

Jack looked at him, his eyes crinkling. "I suppose I'll allow it."

"Lie down on your stomach."

For a moment, Jack's eyes widened. Then he did what he was told. Kin's blood rushed as he breathed deeply and got to his knees beside him. "It's easier to learn this way. You just need to make allowances for the stronger kickback. Really brace the rifle. Right, like that."

He leaned over Jack, checking the alignment of the rifle sight. Oh, the things he wanted to do…

Kin rocked back to his heels and shot to his feet. "There you go. Try it now."

Jack squeezed the trigger, and one of the peach cans went flying with a clatter. Grinning, he hopped to his feet. "Okay, now you try with mine."

"Should I lie down?"

"Uh-huh. Sure." Jack licked his lips.

Kin flattened on his belly in the dry snow and braced himself on his elbows, pressing the rifle against his shoulder. He made sure the clip was locked in place and looked down the sight. He could sense Jack behind him, and a moment later Jack's hand pressed against Kin's lower back.

It was as if Jack's gloves and Kin's parka and layers disappeared, and Kin imagined the feel of Jack's hand against his bare skin. He remembered the taste of Jack's fingers, and *what was wrong with him?* He focused on the remaining peach can, blocking out everything else.

As the can flew into the air, Kin smiled. "Just like shooting womp rats."

Jack laughed and held out a hand to help Kin to his feet. "Imagine having a T-16 out here? Look out, Imperial polar bears."

"I think an X-wing would be better. Balances speed with fire power."

"True. Of course an X-wing is basically a better version of a T-16. And for a big ship, the Millennium Falcon had great manoeuvrability. It wouldn't be bad out here."

Kin grinned. "Fastest hunk of junk in the galaxy. Come on, let's eat. Then you can use the astrocompass." He glanced around. "And we should keep an eye out for bears, of course."

"Where's R2-D2 when you need him? We could get him to do a scan for life forms."

"Maybe we can propose that to CF. I'm sure they'll fund a robot to help us with our patrols." Kin opened a bag of seal meat and some leftover bannock.

Jack laughed as he took a piece of bread. "I'll pull some strings in Ottawa. R2-D2 is definitely an Arctic necessity."

As they ate their lunch and debated which *Star Wars* characters would do the best at Arctic survival (with Chewbacca leading the way due to his fur and strength), Kin wondered how on earth he was going to spend another night in a tent with Captain Jack Turner without kissing him.

IT WAS AFTER MIDNIGHT when Kin stepped outside to piss and scan the area. But the binoculars hung useless around his neck as he stared at the sky. The Aurora Borealis filled him with awe each time he saw it even after all these years. From the horizon to the heavens, the sky was ablaze with green, blue and a hint of pink.

The temperature had dipped to about minus twenty-five, but the wind was still for the moment, as if the spectacle had cast a spell over everything. It was perfectly calm. There was moisture in the air that made him leery—snow might be coming. But for the moment, the only thing that mattered was the wonder filling the sky.

He crouched and poked his head back into the tent. "Jack. Wake up." He nudged Jack's foot.

With a gasp, Jack bolted upright, tumbling onto his side in the confines of the sleeping bag that was pulled up to his ears. He struggled to pull his arms free, and his toque slipped over his forehead. "What is it? Bear?"

"No, nothing like that. Come see."

With his gloves on, Jack fought the zipper on his sleeping bag, and after a moment Kin took off his own gloves and gently knocked Jack's hands away. The zipper was snagged on the neck of Jack's thermal shirt, and Kin shifted to let in more of the light from outside.

Jack tugged the shirt up around his neck, his body tense. Kin's knuckles grazed Jack's throat, and he felt him swallowing hard. When warm breath ghosted across Kin's cheek, his heart skipped a beat.

Then the material came free, and he sat back and escaped the tent. After a minute Jack joined him, zipping up his parka and jamming his feet into his boots. Jack's hat was still askew, and Kin resisted the urge to straighten it.

"Oh my God." Jack stared up, turning all around with his jaw practically scraping the snow beneath their boots. "Northern lights."

"You're lucky—it's a little early for them. I thought you'd want to see."

"Absolutely." Jack grinned, his gaze still locked on the sky. "Thank you." His eyes crinkled, the fine lines fanning out, and the vivid colors washed over his pale skin. His teeth were white and straight, and his face practically glowed.

Kin's groin tightened as desire flowed through him like the hot tea they'd drunk earlier. Jack's expression was soft with childlike awe as he took in the colors soaring above them. Although he knew he should, Kin couldn't seem to turn away.

"Beautiful," Jack murmured.

"Yes," he agreed. As Jack watched the northern lights dance above them, Kin's gaze stayed six feet off the ground.

Chapter Four

W*HY WAS IT so cold?*

The wind was howling, blowing sand into Jack's eyes and mouth through the open windows, and he spat uselessly. But the air was freezing, even with the sun beating down, sending shimmers of heat off the cracked black tarmac. They jolted over a crater in the road, the G-Wagon gears grinding as the corporal behind the wheel navigated the treacherous road. Jack reached for the A/C controls, but couldn't stop the cold. Couldn't roll up the windows either.

They took a bound over a crest in the road, and the landscape came into sickening, familiar focus, the long valley stretching out before them. Jack shuddered, his body shaking as he choked on the sand whirling into the vehicle now. But it was still so fucking cold, and Grant's voice was loud in his ear.

"Is that a kid?"

Gasping, Jack opened his eyes. He stayed rigid,

blinking into the darkness, his heart thumping painfully. *Where the fuck...?* He tried to move, but he was trapped, something binding him. Was he tied? Jesus Christ, did some sand rats get him? He could barely move his arms, and it was so cold, and he was fucking *blind.* He couldn't stop the pathetic whine low in his throat, and he thrashed uselessly.

There was movement somewhere close by, and someone touched his shoulder.

"Get the fuck away from me!"

In the blackness, there was a soft voice. "Jack. It's all right."

He panted harsh and fast, and as light filled the space, he could see the puffs of his breath in the frigid air. Carsen kneeled beside him, sitting back on his heels after lighting the lantern hanging from the top of the tent. His sleeping bag was cast aside in a heap, and he wore his red sweatshirt and uniform pants with his fur slippers. He reached for a white pelt and pulled it around himself.

"It's me. Kin. You're not... You're in the Arctic. Remember?"

"Kin?" Jack's voice was hoarse, his throat raw. "Fuck."

Kin reached into his discarded sleeping bag and pulled out a bottle of water. "Here."

Jack's fingers felt numb, and he struggled in his gloves with the damn zipper on his bag again, but got it down. Sitting up, he took the bottle in both hands so he didn't drop it, and gulped gratefully. He shivered. "Sorry about that."

Kin watched him. "No need." He glanced around as the wind gusted loudly. "Finish the water. I'll melt more." He crawled to the door of the tent.

Jack's pulse still raced, and he concentrated on breathing evenly and sipping the water. He remembered he had his own bottle in his sleeping bag, but he'd almost finished Kin's anyway. He closed his eyes.

"Shit."

"What?" Jack tensed. He squinted at the door, but could only make out the white polar bear fur around Kin's shoulders as Kin blocked the entry.

"Blizzard."

That explained the wind. Keeping himself wrapped tightly in his bag, Jack crawled over and peeked past Kin. He had the impression of movement, and could feel the stinging slaps of snow. "I don't see anything."

With quick movements, Kin zipped shut the outer and inner doors. "That's the problem. It might pass by sunrise."

"And if it doesn't?"

Kin shrugged. "Then we wait." He checked his watch. "It's almost seven. I'll make breakfast."

"Okay. I...thank you." He held up the bottle and added lamely, "For the water."

With a nod, Kin went to work. Jack watched him

light the stove, shivering. The tent shook as a gust of wind shrieked. "Aren't you cold in just your relish suit?"

Kin's brows drew together. "My what?"

"It's what we call the CADPAT." Jack pointed to the camo pants. "Do you have anything on underneath?" As soon as the words left his mouth, he cringed. "I mean…it's just that I'm cold in mine. Long johns don't seem to do much up here. Gloves either." He rubbed his gloved hands together. "Feels so much colder than it was the first night."

"That's because it is. Here." Kin was in front of him again, and he was peeling off Jack's gloves. "Thought your fingers got cold last night because you weren't wearing these. The army should give you proper cold weather gear. These gloves are for shit."

"They're Thinsulate. They're supposed to…" He lost track of what he was saying as Kin took his hands. Jesus, was he going to suck Jack's fingers again? Here in the light? Jack knew he should stop him, but speaking was beyond him.

"You can borrow my spare pair of bear mitts. It's best to wear cotton work gloves underneath. Works better than anything else I've tried. But your gloves will do as long as you put the mitts on top." He started rubbing.

Jack's hands were soon deliciously warm, and he had the strange thought as Kin chafed them that they'd burst into flames, like pieces of wood rubbed together. When Jack looked up, his pulse jumped. Kin was watching him with those intense steel eyes.

"You look like a dog," Jack blurted.

The movement of Kin's hands stuttered, and his eyebrows arched.

Jack's tongue felt thick. "No, I mean…your eyes. They remind me of a husky's. Jesus, I'm sorry. My brain isn't working right now. I feel like I'm still sleeping."

"You're not used to being out in these temperatures. It's called 'cold stupid.' It happens." Kin started rubbing again. "And yes, my grandfather calls me Qimmiq. It's our word for a dog. He means it fondly, of course."

"Does your name mean anything? Kin…"

"Kinguyakkii. It means northern lights. Since my last name is Scottish, my mother wanted to give me an Inuktitut name."

"It's nice." The haze wrapped around Jack's head began to dissipate. Kin's rough hands felt good against his. He had long fingers, and as a new heat pooled in his belly, Jack wondered again what they'd feel like—

Jack jerked his hands away. "It's boiling." He nodded to the stove, where the small pot of ice simmered, filling the tent with delicious warmth.

Kin watched him for a moment before attending to the stove, and Jack lectured himself on the inappropriateness of getting turned on by what amounted to first aid from a subordinate. *That didn't stop you before.* He cast about for something to say. "The Inuit didn't traditionally use surnames, did they?"

"No." Kin opened a tin of what looked like flour, mixing it in the frying pan with some water. "The government used numbers at first. The missionaries had already changed many first names. My mother is Lutaaq. That's her ancient name, but the missionaries called her Ruth. The government gave her a number: E7119. The 'e' meant east. We were either east or west."

"I can't imagine that. Having my identity taken away."

Kin stirred the mixture in the pan. "Me either. In the late sixties an Inuk man went to every Inuit family in the north and asked them to pick a name. They usually chose the name of a respected family member or friend. That's why our first and last names are interchangeable. And some people still have English names."

The smell of baking bannock filled Jack's nose, and he breathed deeply. "Is that still the influence of the missionaries?"

Kin nodded. "TV too. A mix of worlds." He poured boiling water into mugs for tea. "Like me."

"Was that difficult here?" Jack nodded his thanks for the tea and wrapped his hands around it gratefully.

After a long moment, Kin said, "Yes and no. There are a fair number of white people in Nunavut, and no one cared that I was half. But my dad left when I was young, and I guess I felt like there was something missing. That's why I was dying to go away to school."

"You went to the University of Alberta?"

He nodded.

"Is your father back in Edmonton?"

"He's mining in South America. Never stays in one place for long."

"And when you went to school, did you find what was missing?"

Kin's smile was brittle and brief. "Nope. Realized there was too much of me rooted here. I'm not built to be a nomad like my father. My family's here. This is my home."

Jack wanted to ask about Kin's brother, but held his tongue. He was liable to say exactly the wrong thing. Instead he listened to the frigid wind whipping around the tent. It had to be gusting at fifty kilometers at least. "How long do you think it'll last?"

"No way to tell. We'll just have to wait and see." Kin leaned over and rooted around in his pack, pulling out a deck of cards. He held them up with a raised eyebrow.

"Sure. What's your game?"

"Strip Jack Naked."

Jack sputtered and choked on his mouthful of tea. Disbelief and a flare of desire warred in him. He tried for a light tone. "Might be a little cold for that."

Kin was shaking his head, mortification etched on his flushed face. "It's a game my father taught me. I think it's also called Beggar My Neighbor?"

Not sure whether to be disappointed or not, Jack smiled. "I think my brain is sufficiently thawed to handle that. The stove really makes a difference, huh?"

"Yes." Kin gave him an awkward smile before ducking his head.

There was something in his eyes. Was it an answering hunger? Jack had assumed Kin was straight, but the air in the tent felt electric—*new*. Perhaps it was just the storm, or charged particles from the northern lights that lingered somehow. Yet while Kin cut the fresh bannock into chunks, Jack dealt the cards and wondered what kind of game they were really playing.

"STILL SUSFU?"

Kin snorted. "I'm going to assume that means something negative. In which case, yes." He leaned away from the opening of the tent.

The icy air sent a shock over Jack's skin as he crawled over. The world was a blank slate. Somewhere above them the sun was up, but when he extended his arm, his fur mitt completely disappeared into the white. He quickly zipped up the two shells of the tent and joined Kin by the stove. They sat side-by-side on the hides and wrapped furs around themselves, their toques pulled low over their ears. "Must be what, minus forty with the wind-chill?"

"About that."

"Guess we're stuck."

"Or SUSFU, as you would say."

He laughed. "Sorry, I don't realize how often I speak in acronyms until I'm with civvies. Situation unchanged; still fucked up." He thought about what he'd said and quickly added, "Not that you're a civvie."

Kin hitched a shoulder. "Being a reservist isn't the same as serving. I know that."

"It's still important. You're protecting our sovereignty in the Arctic." Jack took off his mitts and gloves underneath before wrapping his hands around his hot metal tea mug again. He'd have to piss very soon if he kept drinking. "Sorry, I sound like a brochure. So tell me, what's your favorite part of being a Ranger?"

"You really want to hear this?"

"I do." He liked listening to Kin talk. There was something soothing about the low rumble of his voice. "But if you don't want to talk about it—"

"No, I do." He smiled softly. "I love being a Ranger. It's one of the best choices I've ever made."

Jack found himself smiling back. "Have you ever spotted a rogue sub?"

"No." Kin laughed. "My cousin in Pond Inlet did a couple of years ago. Reported it right away, and they sent a plane to track it. I found a downed satellite once. Chinese writing on it. Ottawa sent someone to take it away. Most of the time we don't see anything suspicious. Which is a good thing, I suppose. My brother—" He glanced away, suddenly rigid.

For a few moments, Jack didn't say anything. But they were going to be stuck here together for God knew how long, and curiosity won out. Curiosity and an undeniable need to know more about what had caused Kin so much obvious pain. Pain Jack wanted to ease. "Was he older or younger?"

Kin was silent for so long that Jack was about to change the subject and ask about the first thing that popped into his mind—the benefits of tents versus igloos.

"Younger." Kin took a gulp of tea, his eyes on his mug. "By eight years. We had different fathers. His stuck around and married our mother. They're still married now. He's a good man. Always treated me like his own."

Jack watched Kin's profile. His eyelashes fanned out over his cheek as he stared down.

"When my brother was born he screamed so loudly they named him Maguyuk. Howler." Kin smiled fondly. "He was always getting into trouble the way little brothers do."

Jack smiled tentatively. "I'm sure my older sister would have some stories to tell."

"He was always an adventurer. He loved the army cadets program, and he couldn't wait to join the Rangers when he turned eighteen. He had no intention of going south like I did. He was a great hunter. He stayed away from moonshine and all the shit kids can get sucked into. He'd always rather be out on the land than playing video games and huffing gas." Kin was quiet for a moment, his gaze distant. "Me, I dreamed of going away to school. I wanted to live in the city and get to know my father. I couldn't wait to go."

The wind howled, and Jack shivered. He waited for Kin to continue with a growing sensation of dread in the pit of his stomach.

"Do you know how people die in a crevasse?"

Jack blinked. "I...well, they fall."

Kin's gaze was still unfocused. "Yes, sometimes people die from the fall itself. It depends on how deep the crevasse is. Other people survive the fall, but die from the cold. But there's another way."

Jack realized he was holding his breath. His tea had gone lukewarm, and he pulled his gloves and borrowed fur mitts back on. He waited.

"A crevasse is wider at the top. It narrows down as it goes." Kin took off his furry gloves and held his hands up in a V, the heels of his hands pressed together. "People can get wedged in at the bottom. Their legs go through, but then the rest of them is too wide. So they're stuck."

The hair on Jack's neck stood up. "Stuck," he repeated, shuddering.

Kin put his gloves back on and brought his knees to his chest. "With every inhale and exhale, they slip down. Inch by inch, each breath crushes their lungs a bit more. Finally they can't breathe at all."

Although he'd seen some horrible fucking ways to die in the desert, the thought of slowly suffocating in an icy grave made bile rise in Jack's throat. "God. I'm sorry." He wanted to reach for Kin and draw him near, but he didn't.

"Maguyuk was seventeen. Never did get his Rangers sweatshirt. They tried to save him—his friends. But they were too late." Kin inhaled sharply. "If I'd been here…"

"It's not your fault." Jack knew the words were empty, but he didn't have any others. Memories of the steaming desert road crashed through his mind, and his scars itched fiercely. He bared his right hand and scratched at the back of his neck and shoulder, wishing he could reach lower.

"I might have saved him. Or at least…been there. Not two thousand kilometers away."

"Being there isn't always better," Jack said quietly.

Kin looked at him now, his pale eyes intent and sorrowful. "Maybe not, but I'll never know."

Jack did reach for him then, just a hand on Kin's shoulder through all their layers. The moment stretched out, and Jack hadn't wanted to kiss someone so badly in as long as he could remember. He wanted to kiss away the sadness and make Kin smile again. His gaze dropped to Kin's mouth. Kin's lips were lush and slightly chapped at the corners. Only inches separated them, and he would just have to lean over to taste—

Kin shot to his feet, stooping over in the confines of the tent as he dropped his fur and spun around to rummage in a box. "I should call Donald. Let him know we're stuck."

"Uh-huh." Jack concentrated on breathing and keeping his tone normal. The air was thick with a new tension that had descended on them as swiftly as the blizzard. He cleared his throat awkwardly and asked, "You have a shortwave radio, right?"

Kin didn't look at him. "Yes, but I bring my own sat phone. The radio can be unreliable."

He dialed, and a minute later he was speaking Inuktitut, presumably to Donald. Jack felt like an idiot just sitting there. He had to piss, and maybe the frigid conditions would whip some sense back into him. He put on his parka, and was unzipping the outer shell of the tent when Kin grabbed his arm.

"What are you doing?"

"Just going for a piss."

Kin said something else in Inuktitut into the phone and turned it off. "You can't go out alone."

Unreasonable irritation spiked in Jack. "I think I'm capable to going to the bathroom by myself. Been doing it since I was three." He pulled his arm free, the urge to kiss Kin still raring in him like a revving engine going nowhere. He needed a minute to himself to get his head—and dick—back under control.

"You could get disoriented in two steps. That's all it takes." Kin jerked him back from the tent entrance by his arm. "You're not getting lost out there on my watch."

The contrary part of Jack wanted to charge outside anyway, but obviously Kin was right. "So what do I do?"

Kin rooted around in a box and held up a two-liter bottle. "Our very own portable outhouse."

Jack took the bottle, afraid to ask what the procedure was for taking a dump. He made his way through his layers and relieved himself in the bottle on his knees, turning into the corner, the sound of his stream of urine loud in the tent. He ached to stand up and stretch his legs. The tent felt smaller and smaller with each passing hour. "Did Donald know when the weather will clear?"

"By tomorrow, he thinks. It's not as bad up there. All we can do is wait."

"Terrific," Jack muttered. "This mission was a jug fuck from the get-go."

"It's not like I'm having the time of my life stuck here with you either," Kin snapped.

Jack zipped up and screwed on the lid of the plastic bottle. Turning, he saw Kin was shutting off the stove. "It's too cold in here without that."

"We don't know how long we'll be here. Have to conserve fuel. Bundle up." Kin picked up the urine bottle and went to the corner.

The fact that Kin was once again right didn't dampen Jack's irritation. He huffed a little as he sat cross-legged on his sleeping bag. His nerves were rubbed raw with not only the cold—but the stubborn heat coiled low in his belly. Just touching his dick to piss had him twitching and on edge. If he was alone he'd jerk off hard and fast. "Why the fuck would anyone live up here," he muttered.

"If you don't want to be here, why did you come?" Kin's eyes flashed as he whipped around. He was on his knees a few feet away, his jaw tight as he zipped his camo pants.

"I don't want to be anywhere!" Jack yelled, and as the words hung in the cold air, something cracked open inside him, brittle and jagged.

I don't want to be anywhere.

Blinking, Kin sat on his heels.

The fissure widened, and Jack sucked in a breath, words tripping out, slicing his tongue. "The years I was in Afghanistan, I usually wanted to be anywhere else. And now it's over, and what? We won? We lost? What was the point? What changed? Why the fuck did we bother?"

Kin watched him silently.

He wanted to stop them, but the words didn't. "I spent a month in the hospital before I could come home, and when I did, nothing was the same. It was, but it wasn't. My parents still live in the same house in Kanata, but instead of cornfields out back there's another subdivision. Bill and Carol still play rummy every Thursday night with the neighbors down the street, but the Johnsons next door moved out west a few years ago."

Jack scrubbed his face with his fur mitts. He needed to stop rambling, but he couldn't. "My folks kept saying how good it was to have me home. My old room is a generic guest room now, but I laid there staring at the same ceiling I did when I was a dumb kid trying to figure out why I didn't like girls the way my friends did. It was all I could do. Lie there and wonder why the fuck I was still alive and he wasn't."

Jack shuddered, struggling to breathe as he was bombarded with flashes of Grant—*smile, laugh, kisses, resigned sigh*.

Kin still waited with sad eyes.

"It wasn't any better once I went back to my condo downtown in Ottawa. My friends were all glad to have me home, and every weekend they wanted to go out for drinks and dinner in the Market. I went a few times before I started making up excuses. It was easier to stay home with Neville. Dogs don't ask questions." He laughed bitterly. "Grant was allergic to dogs. He wanted to buy a house together when our tour was up, and I used Neville as an excuse every chance I got. Nice, huh?"

Kin opened his mouth, but closed it again without saying anything.

Jack realized he was trembling, and wrapped his arms around himself. "The brass gave me the desk job, and I thought it would be a good change after the sand box. But I hate it. I'm no good at it. They know it and I know it. The colonel sent me here to give me another chance. He shouldn't have bothered. Nothing works anymore. It's all fucked. *I'm* fucked."

The wind shrieked as if in agreement, and the tent shook. Jack squeezed his eyes shut against Kin's sympathetic gaze. *I'm pathetic. Did I just say all that out loud? Fuck me. Fucking fuck.* He scrambled to his knees. "I need to get out of here. I need air. I need—"

His eyes popped open as Kin's arms went around him. Rigid, his breath frozen in his lungs, Jack didn't move. Through their bulky layers, Kin held him, his arms strong and secure. Jack sucked in a breath, pressing his face to Kin's throat. It was warm and rough with stubble, and he gripped Kin's sides, breathing hard.

For a long while, Kin held him and murmured something in Inuktitut, and Jack's pulse slowed as he listened to the rumble of Kin's voice and the rhythm of the words. They had turned off the lantern since the sun was up, but with the driving snow the tent was dim. He closed his eyes.

Stranded on the barren tundra, countless miles from anything except deadly ice and polar bears, he felt *safe*.

Kin must have taken off his gloves, because Jack felt those long fingers against his head, stealing under his toque and rubbing through his short hair. Jack pulled off his hat, eager for more contact, turning into Kin's touch like Neville when he wanted a tummy scratch. *Stop before this goes too far. He's only being kind. He doesn't want this. Doesn't want you.*

Every instinct screamed at him to stay put, but Jack leaned back. He was an army captain—he couldn't cross the line with a subordinate. He met Kin's gaze, and a jolt blazed through him at the darkness in Kin's eyes.

"I want to touch you," Kin said. "If you—"

Jack lunged for Kin's mouth, swallowing the rest of his words with a moan as their lips met and parted, tongues already seeking and exploring. Kin tasted like tea and the iron of the raw seal meat they'd eaten a few hours ago, and Jack reveled in it, his blood stirring as he stroked Kin's tongue with his own.

The stubble on their cheeks rasped together, and Jack yanked off his mitts and Kin's hat so he could tangle his fingers in Kin's short, thick hair.

They were wearing far too many clothes, and Jack tugged and struggled to touch flesh. He growled as he encountered another layer, and Kin broke the kiss, laughing. His eyes were alight, and he held Jack's face in his hands to kiss him again soundly.

He whispered against Jack's lips. "Best way to stay warm is skin to skin."

Jack wanted to say something clever, but all he could manage was, "*Yes.*" He licked across Kin's lower lip.

Getting their clothes off took a frustratingly long time, and when Jack reached his final thermal shirt, he hesitated. His fingers gripped the hem, and he didn't move. The light was murky enough that Kin probably wouldn't even see, but his heart still skipped. He was naked from the waist down, and he needed to just rip off the shirt and get under the blankets.

Kin was naked, and he was zipping their sleeping bags together and *good God.* Jack forgot about his scars and everything else as he took in Kin's gorgeous body. Under his Ranger uniform he was lean and muscular, and a dark trail of hair led down from his bellybutton to his thick, uncut cock. It was hard, and Jack's mouth watered at the thought of filling his mouth with it as it swelled.

"Jack?"

Blinking, he realized Kin was frowning at him. Likely because Jack was still wearing his shirt, and was clutching the hem so tightly the material had ripped. He flushed to the tips of his ears at the thought of Kin seeing how ugly he was when Kin was so breathtaking. "I…" Might as well spit it out. "There are scars. It's fine." With a deep breath, he shrugged out of the shirt and shimmied beneath Kin into their joint sleeping bag.

Then they were naked together, the pelts and furs under them soft against Jack's head. The marks that rained down Jack's back were hidden from sight, and he let himself stop worrying as he tasted Kin's mouth again, Kin a welcome weight on top of him.

The air felt wet in their cocoon as they kissed and rutted together, skin getting slick. Jack had started getting hard the moment their lips first met, and now he was straining against his belly, a jolt of fire sparking through him every time his cock rubbed against Kin's throbbing flesh. After being so cold, now Jack couldn't imagine it, his body thrumming with fever.

He bit back a moan as Kin ducked down to lick and suck Jack's nipples. Neither of them had much hair on their chests, and Jack ran his hands over

Kin's smooth skin, touching everywhere he could reach as he bucked up against Kin's hips.

Kin groaned. "Good," he muttered. "Good."

Their harsh pants were loud, and Jack barely recognized his own needy cries. He was leaking, and he needed release. Wrapping one leg around Kin's hip, he arched up. "Please," he croaked.

As Kin licked his palm and took Jack's cock in his hand, Jack thought he might come right there. His toes curled, his muscles clenching. He kissed Kin messily, their teeth clashing. Their pants filled his ears in the cocoon of sleeping bags and furs, and Kin was shadowed above him, holding himself up on his elbow as he jerked Jack with a firm grip, his thumb sliding over the slit.

"You're cut," he muttered. "I was wondering. I like it."

Jack stared into Kin's silvery eyes in the murky light, gasping and thrusting up into his hand. The wind and the storm and the rest of the world was gone, and this was everything—the touch of Kin's hand and the warmth of his breath as he murmured encouragement.

With a gasp, Jack came in long spurts. He opened his mouth, shuddering with each pulse, the release so intense that colors swam before his eyes the way they did when they lit up the Arctic sky.

Chapter Five

K IN DRAGGED HIS TONGUE over Jack's stomach and chest, savoring the musky flavor as he licked up the semen. There was no cloth or anything that would do the job in reach, and it had been so long since he'd tasted the salty tang of sex. Jack was still shuddering with aftershocks as Kin lazily stroked him. He expected to wake up any moment, but it seemed that no—this was real.

He and Captain Jack Turner were having sex.

His cock ached, and he rubbed against Jack's hip as he licked his fingers clean where a few drops had dripped down. Jack's puff of breath tickled his head, and Kin glanced up to find Jack watching him with dark eyes and lips parted.

"You need...you..."

Kin swirled his tongue around Jack's index finger slowly. "What?" he teased, smiling at Jack's lack of coherency.

"You need to come." Jack tugged on Kin's shoulders.

At this, he could only nod, because *yes.* He moved back up to kiss Jack deeply, their tongues winding together as Kin rubbed against him. He expected Jack to jerk him off, but Jack was still urging him upward.

"In my mouth." It was a breathy command.

As his balls tightened, Kin was afraid he wouldn't last long enough to get there. The thought of Jack sucking his dick—and hearing him say the words—made his body hum and even more of his blood rush south. He was all desperation and need, his movements awkward as he clambered up to feed Jack his cock.

The sleeping bag slipped down his shoulders as he straddled Jack's head with his knees, but he barely felt the change in temperature. Jack was eager for it, opening his mouth wide as Kin surged between his lips. The wet heat that enveloped him had him crying out, and he braced himself on one hand over Jack's head, the other tangling in Jack's hair as he fucked his mouth.

For years he'd been on his own, and he'd actually forgotten how good it could be to have another man's mouth on him. Kin's grunts filled the tent, along with the wet slurps as Jack sucked him deeply, opening so beautifully, his thin lips stretched and saliva dripping down his chin.

Kin made sure not to choke him, only going so

deep before drawing back and pushing in again. Jack's short nails raked over Kin's thighs and hips, his nostrils flaring. Electricity raced through Kin, the juxtaposition of hot around his cock and cold on his bare skin heightening the sensations and making it all seem more real. More intense. It felt so damn good, and he wanted to stay here forever.

But it wasn't long before he tensed, his hips stuttering. "I'm going to…"

Jack didn't push him away, and he swallowed every burst as pleasure burned through Kin, spreading from his cock and balls to the tips of his fingers and toes. Gasping, he spent himself until he was soft. He slipped out of Jack's mouth and squirmed back down, pulling the sleeping bag back over them tightly.

He sprawled half across Jack with their legs tangled. Jack's mouth was shiny with spit, his lips red and debauched. Kin ran his thumb over Jack's bottom lip and kissed him gently, tasting himself there.

Jack's short hair stuck up, and Kin murmured, "*Nini,*" as he smoothed it down. In answer to Jack's knit brows, he added, "Porcupine." It seemed fitting in more ways than one.

Smiling, Jack rubbed their noses together. "That's the only Inuktitut I know. Eskimo kiss. Although I know I shouldn't use that word. Inuit kiss?"

Kin felt loose and wonderfully spent, warm in their little world of sleeping bags and furs. "*Kunik*, it's called. It's not what Hollywood thinks it is—rubbing noses together."

"Oh? What is it?"

Pressing his nose and upper lip to Jack's cheek, Kin inhaled deeply. "It's a way to remember a loved one," he murmured. "Breathe them in and know them again. Parents and children. Lovers." He leaned back and propped his head on his hand, rolling onto his hip so he wasn't too heavy on Jack. He ran his foot up and down Jack's shin. "It's not a sexual thing."

His breath shuddering, Jack shook his head. "Could've fooled me." He traced his fingers over Kin's side. "So, I assume you're gay or bi. Unless this is an Arctic thing. Catch your kisses where you can?"

Kin laughed. "No. I mean yes—I'm gay. You?"

"Yep. Came out when I graduated high school."

Kin couldn't help but be a little jealous at that freedom. "What did your family say?"

"There was an adjustment period, but they accepted it. What's it like up here being gay?"

Painful. It was the first thing that popped into Kin's head, quickly followed by *lonely.* But he shrugged. "It is what it is."

Jack ran his finger over Kin's cheekbone. "What does that mean?"

He sighed. "I don't know. It's not really accepted

here. It's more controversial than it is down south."

"Why do you think that is?"

"The influence of the Christian missionaries is a big part of it. But it's our own tradition as well. They raised the rainbow flag at Iqaluit city hall during the Olympics in Russia, and some folks put up a stink about how it's not Inuit custom to be gay. There's not word for it in Inuktitut."

Jack frowned. "Which doesn't mean it didn't happen."

"No. It had to happen. Some scholars say it did and wasn't an issue. Men out hunting, women staying behind together. But..." Kin swallowed hard. "To not even have the language to express it makes it feel shameful. The idea of people living together as a couple and being out—that's a southern notion. Our traditions, our history—it's about survival, and having children is part of that. In the Arctic, survival is what matters."

"But obviously you're not the first gay Inuit."

"It's Inuk when it's singular." He winced. "Sorry. It's the teacher in me."

"No, correct me on stuff like that when I'm wrong. It happens once in a blue moon. Me being wrong, I mean." Jack's eyes crinkled.

"A rare occurrence, I'm sure," Kin teased. "And no, I'm obviously not the first or only. Support is growing, but it's a slow process."

"Are you out in Arctic Bay?"

The thought made his heart skip. "No. My mother's the only one who knows. My grandfather and stepfather…they wouldn't like it."

Jack frowned. "That must be difficult. What does she say?"

The memory of her glistening eyes and tight press of lips was etched in Kin's mind like one of the soapstone tchotchkes she carved for tourists. The way she'd holed up with her bible as if there was a solution there. "Nothing. I'm her only child now, so I suppose there's not much she can say. I know she wants me to be happy, and she worries about me. Worries I'll lose my job if people found out. Lose my role in the Rangers."

"CF doesn't have a problem with it. I serve openly."

"I know. But Rangers are community groups. I was elected sergeant, and I'd have to step down if they knew. No one would respect me. Especially the older men and women."

"You don't know that, though. People can surprise you."

"I do know it," Kin insisted, tensing. "I know this place. You don't."

Jack stopped stroking Kin's chest. "I'm sorry. You're right."

Exhaling a long breath, Kin shook his head. "Believe me, I've thought a lot about it. It's best for me if I keep it to myself."

"Okay." Jack caressed him again. "So why stay? What's holding you here? Why did you return after you left?"

Turning onto his back, Kin stared at the ceiling of the tent, which wavered in the wind. He should turn the stove back on, but he was so content with Jack pressed against him in their nest that he didn't want to move. *What's holding me here?* It was a question he'd been trying to answer for years now.

"When my brother died, I'd just finished teacher's college. I came back to be with my family, and I got a job at the school on a short-term contract. One of the teachers had taken an extended sick leave. But she never came back, and somehow I just…stayed." He could feel Jack's intent gaze on him, but he didn't meet it.

"But why?"

"I can't explain it. There's something about the land that calls to me. Sings in my blood and fills my heart with every beat." He closed his eyes. "Despite all the reasons I should go, that's why I stay." He met Jack's gaze. "Cheesy and stupid, I know."

But Jack didn't smile. "No. That's what home should be." He burrowed closer, resting his head on Kin's chest.

The warmth blooming through Kin wasn't only from their shared body heat. But when he stroked down Jack's back, his fingers bumped over raised, damaged skin. Jack tensed, inhaling sharply.

Before Jack could pull away, Kin wrapped his arms around him. He couldn't see the scars in their cocoon, and he didn't touch them again. He didn't ask either, for that was a question for another day. As he played with the points of Jack's hair, Jack eventually breathed evenly again.

Kin was dozing off when Jack's voice rumbled against him, his breath hot on Kin's chest.

"What about dating? How do you handle that up here?"

"I don't. I had a few boyfriends in Edmonton. Nothing serious. But here, there's no one for me."

"Isn't it lonely? Not that I've done any dating since I've been back. But still."

"I don't mind." *Lie.* "I have plenty to keep me busy." *Truth.* "There's more to life." *Undetermined.*

Jack kissed Kin's neck, his hand skimming down over Kin's belly. "Yes, but sometimes it's…nice, isn't it?" He sucked on the tender skin by Kin's collarbone. "To feel this."

Kin pulled Jack on top of him. "Yes," he murmured, before licking into Jack's mouth. They both moaned softly as they kissed and moved against each other, finding an easy rhythm to the music of the keening wind.

He hoped the snow would fall for some time yet.

"I CAN SEE the world again," Jack called from the door of the tent. "Of course the sun is already setting." He scooted back in, zipping the doors before huddling in front of the stove. "I guess we should just stay here for another night, huh?"

After all night and most of the day in the tent, Kin itched to get outside and move. "It's *tatkresiwok* tonight," he said, adding, "Full moon. It'll rise soon, and if the sky's clear we can travel to the coast this evening. Camp there." He caught the flash of disappointment on Jack's face, and something warm and tender bloomed in him. He zipped up his parka and crawled over.

It felt so easy and right to draw Jack into a deep kiss, and Jack moaned into him, opening his mouth. When they both caught their breath, Kin whispered in his ear, "Don't worry. We'll have plenty of time in the tent later tonight."

Jack shuddered, smiling. "I'll hold you to that, Sergeant."

"I have to follow your orders, Captain." He nipped Jack's earlobe.

But Jack jerked away, his mouth a thin line. "Don't say that."

"I was only kidding." Kin sat back on his heels, mystified by the sudden shift in Jack's mood.

Yanking down his toque, Jack sighed. "But I still shouldn't be doing this. We both know that."

"It's only between us. CF never has to know. It's

not as if you used your rank to force me into anything." Kin pulled on his own hat and gloves, trying to keep the disappointment burning in him from affecting his voice. "But if you want, we can put an end to it right now."

Keeping his head down, Jack fiddled with the zip on his parka. "I should say yes. But it would be a lie." He glanced up, his eyes bright, breath coming heavier. "All I want is to feel your body again. Taste your mouth, and your skin, and your cock. I want to stay in this tent and fuck until we run out of food and fuel, and have to leave. That's what I want."

Kin swallowed thickly. Why not? Getting back to the coast could wait. He and Jack stared at each other, their breath fogging the air. Kin was getting hard just thinking of all the things they could do. He thought he could fuck and talk with Jack for days and still want more. His voice had gone hoarse. "I could call Donald and tell him we're staying the night for some reason. He wouldn't—"

The sat phone's shrill ring filled the tent, and Kin's heart thumped. He answered, and Donald spoke as if conjured by some sort of magic.

"One of the German tourists wandered off in Sirmilik. South end. We're heading out. Pond Inlet patrol too. But you might be closer."

"What were they doing out there today?"

"Weather cleared, and they apparently insisted. They're on the peninsula. South of the big valley, and east of the ridge. On the glacier fields. I'll call back when I have exact coordinates."

"Got it. On our way."

Jack was already packing up the last of their gear, all business. "What's the situation? SAR?"

"Yes." Kin didn't tease him about the acronym for search and rescue. They had to move.

He filled him in as they took down the tent, and soon they were back on the snowmobile. The sun was below the horizon, with the moon rising across the tundra as Kin started the engine. His breath caught as Jack wrapped his arms around him. Even through all their layers, Kin imagined he could feel the heat of Jack's body, the power of his thighs snug against Kin's hips.

The longing to turn just for a moment to kiss Jack again was a wave he braced against. No—they had a job to do. There would be another time for kissing. With the komatik trailing behind, they started off across the land, and Kin hoped that time would be soon.

IT WAS JUST after midnight as they reached the area of the park where the German woman had last been seen. The clear sky had fortunately offered plenty of moonlight to guide their way across the tundra. Although they were on a mission, Kin couldn't help but feel a moment of peace every now and then at the tightness of Jack's arms around him, and the solid warmth of his body.

He found himself hoping the other Rangers had found the tourist already—certainly for her sake as well. But selfishly so he and Jack could continue their patrol. So they could spend another night in their own world of the tent. He wanted to work Jack into a frenzy and then see the two lines on his forehead smoothed out in peacefulness after he came.

And he wanted to talk with him. He wanted to curl up together for as long as they could and find out everything there was to know. Kin shook his head to himself as he skirted the snowmobile around a hill he knew to be rocky beneath the layer of snow. This wasn't like him.

"Everything okay?" Jack shouted.

Kin nodded and adjusted his clear goggles. He needed to concentrate on the mission, but after a minute his mind wandered again. In Edmonton, the guys he'd hooked up with had been fun. Until they hadn't been, and that's when Kin would go his own way. He'd never gotten too close. What was the point? It wasn't as if he could bring a lover to Arctic Bay.

Even before Maguyuk's death had yanked him back to Nunavut, he'd always known deep down that he couldn't stay away. He'd known that to go home, he'd have to be alone.

Yet with Jack, he found himself wanting to know more. Wanting to burrow inside the way he did a sleeping bag on an Arctic night. He wanted to know the story of the scars on Jack's body and his soul. He wanted to help them fade, and talk about the stars and see Jack's face light up like a boy's when he used the astrocompass. He wanted to find out what else would make Jack's eyes crinkle that way.

Kin fought the urge to shake his foolish head again. In a couple of days, Jack would be returning to the south, never to return. It was ridiculous to even entertain this…what? Crush? He had a good job and a good life. He'd accepted the fact that romance wouldn't be a part of that life. Couldn't be. He needed to put a stop to this dangerous thinking.

He and Captain Jack Turner had fucked, and it had been a good way to pass the time in the whiteout. That was all it was.

The end.

They were nearing the glacier fields where the Germans had been skiing. It was late in the season for tourists to be skiing the park since travel by water would soon be impossible as the freeze up happened, but the Germans had apparently paid a couple of guides from Arctic Bay handsomely to take them to the park by snowmobile.

Kin was just about to stop and check the GPS when a *clank* echoed from the engine. He cut the power, and he and Jack climbed off into the dry snow. It was about minus twenty, but the wind was calm. He scanned the area, but didn't detect any movement in the moonlight. Still, he handed Jack the Enfield from the front of the komatik. Bears could have heard their approach and be coming to investigate.

"Do you know why it would make that sound?" Jack asked, pulling off his goggles.

Shaking his head, Kin unhooked the komatik and heaved the snowmobile on its side. "I'm going to take a look just in case. Sometimes chunks of ice can ding the engine."

"You know how to fix these things?"

With a nod, Kin took off his goggles and squatted in the snow. "Can't call CAA out here. We all know how to fix engines."

"School teacher by day. Ranger and ace mechanic by weekend. Not to mention astronomer."

Kin smiled as he flicked on his flashlight and leaned in to examine the piston. "Something like that. Can you get my toolbox from the front of the komatik? The sled, I mean."

The snow crunched under Jack's boots, and a minute later he returned with the tools. Kin pulled off his grizzly mitts, wearing just his cotton work gloves as he took a wrench to one of the bolts. "This is a new snow machine," he grumbled. "Shouldn't be acting up already."

Jack crouched, propping the rifle against the

snowmobile. "They don't build things like they used to, that's for damn sure. I can't count how many times our equipment broke down in the desert. All that sand is hell on mechanisms."

"Maybe I should go back to a dog sled." Kin ducked his head to get a better look at one of the gears. "It all looks fine. I'll tighten a few of these bolts just in case."

"Do you get called out on many SARs?"

Kin couldn't resist this time. "Did you ever meet an acronym you didn't like?"

"Nope. It's the best thing about the military. More acronyms than I dreamed possible."

"What's your favorite?" Kin tightened a bolt.

Jack thought about it for a moment. "LBRT."

"Which is?"

"Little black rubber thingy."

Laughing, Kin shook his head. "Shut up."

"I'm serious! We use them to tie down tarps on our vehicles. Hey, did you…?"

Kin's head was still down. "Hmm?" He fiddled with the machinery.

"Hello!" Jack's voice was suddenly distant.

With a jolt, Kin was on his feet, but Jack was already twenty feet away. "Jack! Stop!"

"I can hear her! This way, come on!" Jack raced on.

"Goddamn it, stop! Jack!" Kin grabbed his mitts and raced after him. "Get back here!" He clenched his jaw as he ran. *Stubborn man.* "I said stop right there!"

For a split second, Jack actually did. Then he was gone, swallowed by the land in a single, silent gulp.

Chapter Six

*D*ARK. *HURT. HELP!*
He'd stopped falling. That was something, at least. Jack was almost sideways in the narrowing gap between the walls of ice. His heart pounded painfully, adrenaline roaring through him like white water. He gasped for air.

I'm in my grave.

Panic tightened his lungs, and he cried out pitifully into the silence. *No, no, no! Not like this!* He had to focus. Squeezing his eyes shut, which was pointless in the darkness, he concentrated on breathing as deeply as he could. The stars in his vision faded, and he opened his eyes again. The cold air burned his throat, but he took it in steadily.

Okay. Stop. Assess.

His right shoulder was jammed painfully into one side, his scars screaming as if his flesh was ripped open again even though he knew it wasn't. When he tentatively wiggled his right leg, it was hanging into the void. His left arm was free, but his left leg was bent at a bad angle. His knee throbbed, but at least it had stopped him from falling farther. If both of his legs had gone in, he'd be suffocating like Kin's brother.

Panic surged, but subsided as he remembered Kin was up there. He knew without a shred of doubt that Kin would get him out. But it was so cold, and if he fell any farther…

"Jack!"

Relief flooded him at the sound of Kin's voice. Gingerly, he tilted his head back, blinking into the beam of a flashlight. He couldn't tell how far up Kin was, and prayed he hadn't fallen too deep.

"Don't move. I've got you."

But when the light disappeared and he saw the outline of Kin in the moonlight, Jack realized the ground was at least twenty feet up.

"Are you hurt?" Kin called down.

"No. Not really." His voice sounded too loud.

Did I hit my head? He lifted his left hand to prod at his skull, but didn't feel any bumps through the layers of his mitts and hat. Pressing his lips together, he shifted to relieve the pressure on his bent leg and try to get it at a better angle—

As his yelp reverberated, he slid another few inches. Blood rushed in his ears, and his knee jammed into a worse spot. His muscles and tendons screamed, but he stayed motionless.

"Jack!"

"I'm okay." His throat felt as though he'd swallowed sand.

"I've got you. Okay? Don't move. I'm setting the anchor for the rope."

Trapped in the narrow chasm, Jack's mind spun back over how he'd managed to land here. *The German.* He'd heard the cries and started running, certain the missing woman was close at hand. He'd registered Kin's shouts just as the snow had given way, revealing the rift in the glacier as he plummeted into it helplessly.

"She's close. You should look for her first." There was no reply—only the echoes of Kin's harsh breathing. "Kin?"

"I heard you," he called. "She could be miles away. You're right here. I'm getting you out."

"No, I heard her. It was clear as day. She's close," Jack shouted.

"You can't always believe your ears up here. Your eyes either. The Arctic plays tricks. I've heard men talking a mile away, their voices carrying right across the land as if they were next to me. That's why we don't run off half cocked."

Really shit the bed on this one. "Goddamn," he murmured.

Closing his eyes again, Jack breathed in and out. The pain in his right shoulder warred with his left knee, and even in his mitts and boots, his fingers and toes were starting to go numb. It was like going into a cold basement, the temperature even lower here than at the frigid surface. With slow, careful movements, he tugged his neck warmer up over as much of his face as he could. His teeth were chattering.

Think of somewhere warm.

Of course the first damn place that filled his mind, expanding into every corner, was Afghanistan. That day replayed in his mind like a DVD he couldn't pause or fast forward. All he could do was rewind and watch it over and over again.

He wiped the back of his hand across his mouth, wishing he could spit out the constant grit on his tongue. Even in the G-Wagon with the windows rolled up and AC blasting, sweat dripped into his eyes from under his helmet. In the driver's seat beside him, Corporal Gagnon nattered on about his girlfriend back in Montreal.

"So then she says we've grown apart. Va chier! I thought she was the one. Said she'd wait while I was over here." He snorted. "Didn't even make it a year. You know—"

In the sudden silence, Jack asked, "Know what?" He glanced at Gagnon, who sat up straighter, peering intently through the windshield.

Jack tensed. "What is it?"

From the backseat, Grant said, "Is that a kid?"

Gagnon took his foot off the gas, and they all leaned forward. They were at the head of the convoy, and Jack radioed for the others to hang back. He didn't need to pull out his binoculars to know that it was indeed a kid on the road, but he got a closer look anyway. Little girl. Weeping. He scanned the area for any sign of movement. Nothing.

"Give us fifty feet."

Gagnon stopped the G-Wagon as ordered. The girl just stood in the middle of the empty road, sobbing. The black tarmac had to be burning her bare feet, but maybe she was used to it. Jack mentally flicked through their options. They could drive around her, but wasn't the whole point of being there to help little Afghani girls?

Private Sagemiller was in the back next to Grant, and it was on the tip of Jack's tongue to order Sagemiller out to see what was wrong with the kid. But he snapped his jaw shut. Even thought he and Grant were still on the downlow, he couldn't show any favoritism. "McKenzie. Check it out."

Under his breath, Grant muttered, "Now I'm a terp?" as he opened the vehicle door.

"Just check it out." Jack cringed at the blast of hot air, irritation bubbling up. No matter what he and Grant were to each other in their free time—and just what they were was up for debate—he was the commanding officer.

Sagemiller cleared his throat. "Terp, sir?"

The kid was a total cornflake, and asked questions every five minutes. Jack took a deep breath and made sure he didn't let his frustration with Grant show. It wasn't Sagemiller's fault. "Civilian interpreter. We don't have one with us today." The radio crackled with a query from one of the other G-Wagons, and Jack picked it up. "Stand by to stand by."

He watched Grant slowly approach the girl, who looked to be about eight or nine. Raising the binoculars, Jack did another sweep of the area. There was nothing. But a growing sense of dread was building in him, a buzz growing louder. "Something's not right." He opened the door and hopped out. "McKenzie! Fall back!"

But Grant kept going, within ten feet of the child now.

"McKenzie! I said fall back!"

Even at a distance, he could spot the anger in Grant's rigid shoulders. Instead of following orders, Grant took another step toward the girl. Swearing under his breath, Jack broke into a jog along the cracked road. Fuck, he should have known better than to ever get involved with another soldier, let alone his lieutenant. Grant was pissed about that morning, and now he was letting it affect the job. That was it. Jack was ending it as soon as they got back to base.

"McKenzie, don't get any closer!"

"Captain!" It was Gagnon's voice.

Jack stopped and turned back.

Then he was flying, and the air was fire.

"Jack? Answer me!"

Blinking, he peered up. Kin's face was in shadow, backlit by the moon. "Yes. I'm here." His teeth weren't chattering anymore, but he had a feeling that was a bad sign.

"I'm lowering the harness. You've got to get it over your head and under your arms."

Okay.

"Jack!"

He realized he hadn't spoken aloud. "Okay." He was feeling numb all over, the pain in his twisted knee and shoulder fading, the phantom cries of his scars silent once more.

"It's there. Can you see it?" The flashlight illuminated the crevasse.

"Yeah."

The rope was blue and thick, and he reached through the loop with his left hand. Getting the harness over his head wasn't too hard. But now he had to get it under his right arm as well without falling deeper.

"That's it. You're doing great."

The increased pressure on Jack's left knee made his eyes water, and he tried to reach up and grip the rope with his left hand for enough leverage to free his right shoulder from the ice wall. But his fingers didn't want to obey. He shoved, but it was no good.

He was opening his mouth to say that he couldn't do it when his left leg gave way, and he was falling again.

The rope jerked him to a stop, and he gasped, adrenaline bursting through the numbness. The walls of ice touched his waist on both sides, and the rope dug into the right side of his neck. It was unbearably tight under his left arm, and he fought to keep his arm down. If he raised it, the harness would come free and he'd be wedged. It already hurt to breathe.

"I've got you."

Jack listened to Kin's voice, imagining it was Kin's arms around him instead of the harness.

"Just raise your right arm and squeeze it under the harness. You can do it."

The throbbing of his shoulder matched the thumping of his heart as Jack did as he was told. *Kin's got me. He won't let me fall.*

"There. Now just stay as still as you can."

The only sounds were the creak of the rope and Jack's stuttered breath loud in his own ears. Inch by inch, Kin hoisted Jack toward the surface. Slowly, slowly, the moonlight got closer. Jack looked down, and there was only a black void.

The edge of the crevasse dug into Jack's back as he was hauled over the side, but the relief blocked out any pain. He blinked at the stars, wanting to tell Kin how grateful he was, but unable to do more than groan.

Panting, Kin dragged him farther, not stopping until they were back by the snowmobile. Jack tried to say that he was fine, but the words seemed frozen on his tongue. He closed his eyes, listening to Kin bustle around. Kin spoke in Inuktitut, evidently to someone on the sat phone, so Jack didn't try to answer. Then there was wonderful warmth on his face, and he blinked.

Kin was there, his breath puffing out over Jack's cheeks. Then he was dragging Jack again, this time into the tent, which he'd somehow put up already. It occurred to Jack that time was passing strangely, and maybe he'd hit his head after all. What he really wanted most of all was to sleep…

"Jack!" Kin's voice was too loud.

He tried to tell him that as Kin pulled off Jack's clothes. It was too cold, but then Kin was naked as well, and they were in the double sleeping bag, and Jack's skin prickled where Kin rubbed him. The pain in his knee and shoulder returned with a vengeance as he warmed up, Kin's breath and flesh like a furnace in their sleeping bag. The haze in his mind began to dissipate, and Jack focused on Kin above him, breathing heavily as he methodically rubbed Jack's body from top to bottom, going over each finger and toe.

"Guess you got to play Strip Jack Naked after all."

Kin's pale gaze shot up to meet Jack's. After a

moment, his shoulders relaxed, and he smiled. "I suppose I did."

"Sorry. I thought… Just ran without thinking."

For a few moments, Kin ran his finger over the planes of Jack's face, examining him with a serious expression. He pressed his nose and upper lip to Jack's cheek and inhaled deeply.

Jack could feel the tickle of stubble above Kin's lip, and he held his breath. Was it possible that at the beginning of the week they'd never even met? Now he never wanted to let go. Jack clung to Kin, swallowing thickly.

"Your instinct is to help," Kin murmured. "That's not a bad thing."

"The German—we should…" Jack tried to push himself up with his left hand.

"They found her. Frostbitten, but she'll be fine. She had good equipment and burrowed in for the night. How do you feel? Are you injured?" Kin smoothed his hand gently over Jack's arm.

"Wrenched my knee and shoulder. They don't feel broken. Some ice should do the trick." He laughed. "On second thought, maybe some ibuprofen."

With a smile, Kin kissed him softly. "In a little while we'll head back to Arctic Bay. Get the doc to check you out in the morning. I want to make sure you get warm enough first."

Jack urged Kin fully on top of him, spreading his

legs. His knee and shoulder hurt, but it was worth it. "I think if you kiss me, it'll help."

Caressing Jack's hair, Kin smiled. "You think so, Nini?"

He nodded, feeling ridiculous pleasure at the nickname.

Kin pressed their lips together, kissing him with a gentleness that made Jack ache in a brand new way.

JACK'S STOMACH TIGHTENED at the quiet knock on the door, and he bounded off the bed, sending a few of the report pages he had spread across the duvet fluttering to the floor. He ignored the flare of pain as his knee protested, and with a deep breath, he straightened his T-shirt and brushed off his green field uniform trousers. There was a little hole in the big toe of his left sock, but he didn't have time to put on his boots.

Then he wiped the foolish grin off his face, hoping it wouldn't be Susan from the front desk checking on him again. Not that he didn't appreciate her concern, but there was only one person he wanted to see. He cleared his throat. "Coming." He opened the door, and his heart leapt.

Kin wore his Ranger uniform without a coat. Beneath the brim of his red baseball cap, his pale eyes were intent. They stared at each other for a few heartbeats. There had been so many things Jack wanted to say, but now that Kin was actually in front of him, the words evaporated. Jack remembered to let him inside, and Kin stood by the closed door with his hands clasped behind him. They stared at each other again.

In the tent it had all been so easy—gentle kisses and touches as Jack had warmed up again. Just being close to Kin had felt better than he'd imagined possible. But now back in what passed for the real world, it was like a force field had suddenly activated between them.

"How do you feel?" Kin asked.

"Fine. Sore, but it's nothing. Strained my knee and shoulder, and there are a few bumps and bruises. I thought—" Jack stopped himself, but what the hell. "I thought you might come back to visit this afternoon. After you finished up with the Germans and all that."

Kin's expression brightened. "Did you want me to come back? I didn't think it would be appropriate now that…well, now. Here."

This is your out. "It isn't. You're right. It's entirely inappropriate."

Nostrils flaring, Kin jerked his head in a nod and cleared his throat. "Right. So, we should set a time for Nanisivik. Donald's lending me his truck. We can drive there whenever you want. I guess your flight's tomorrow morning, right? So we should go tonight. If you still want to."

"I want to."

"Okay." Kin's gaze was locked on the thin brown carpet.

"I wanted you to come back. I still want you. I don't care what's appropriate. I should, but I don't. I—"

His words were cut off as Kin closed the distance between them in a blink, kissing him soundly. He tossed his cap to the floor and held Jack's face in his hands, and smiled against his mouth. "I was afraid you'd say no. And you needed your rest."

"All rested now," Jack muttered. "I'll live. Thanks to you."

"You almost…" Kin shook his head, looking down. He dropped his hands to his sides.

"But I didn't. You saved me." When Kin didn't meet his gaze, Jack inched closer. "Kin?"

Kin's voice was barely a whisper. "I couldn't save my brother. I was so afraid I wouldn't save you either. That I'd be there this time, but I'd have to watch you die. That I'd fail again."

"Hey, look at me. You didn't fail either of us." Jack caressed Kin's cheek, kissing him gently.

"I heard his voice out there. I know that sounds crazy. But I felt like he was there, helping me tie the knots in the rope. Giving me the strength to pull you up. When I think of him now, it's…not so hollow. It doesn't make any sense, but…"

"Makes perfect sense." Jack kissed him again. "I knew you'd save me. I never doubted it, not for a second."

Smiling softly, Kin took hold of Jack's hands. "Really?"

"Really."

They pressed their foreheads together, just breathing for a minute, leaning into each other, fingers entwined.

"Now come here. If we're going to break the rules, might as well go big." Jack tugged Kin toward the spare bed. He couldn't hide his wince as he fell back on the mattress and his shoulder twinged.

Still on his feet, Kin immediately pulled back, his brow furrowed. "Are you sure you're not hurt?"

"*Yes.*" Jack sat on the edge of the bed, taking Kin's hands again and pulling. "I survived an IED. I can handle a fall."

But Kin resisted, stroking Jack's hands with his thumbs. "Jack…"

He recognized the familiar pity in Kin's eyes, and shot to his feet despite the flare of pain, shoving away from the bed. "It's fine. Forget it. If you don't want to, I have work to do." He stood by the bed closest to the bathroom and began rifling through the papers strewn there. The tightness in his chest was familiar as well. He tensed as Kin's breath ghosted across the back of his neck, and his hands rested on Jack's shoulders.

At first, Kin didn't say anything, and Jack breathed shallowly through parted lips. Kin nuzzled against Jack's head as he lightly stroked down Jack's arms, his callused hands leaving warmth in their wake. Jack's skin tingled, and he leaned back into Kin, a sigh escaping as Kin stole his hands under Jack's T-shirt.

His fingertips skimmed over Jack's belly and chest, barely touching his nipples. Jack's excitement grew with each gentle, teasing sweep, and he closed his eyes. He wouldn't be able to stand much longer, all the tension draining away as his dick swelled. He wanted to flop back on the bed and spread his legs, offering anything Kin wanted of him.

Then his breath stuttered and his eyes opened. Kin's hands were on his back under the cotton, touching the scars. Jack's body vibrated, but no longer with desire. "Don't." His brain said to pull away, but he couldn't seem to move.

"It's all right," Kin whispered, kissing the side of Jack's neck. "Can I?" He slid his palms down Jack's sides to the hem of the T-shirt.

Breath coming fast now, Jack's pulse raced. He'd only met the man days ago, but somehow he trusted that Kin wouldn't hurt him. He nodded. He didn't want Kin to see how ugly he was, but somehow part of him did. For the first time since that day in the long desert valley, he wanted to be seen.

Kin lifted the hem, and Jack raised his arms. As

he lowered them, his heart thumped. Closing his eyes, he waited for the shocked intake of breath from Kin. He waited for the rejection, and the judgment, because it was his fault. Grant was dead and Jack was alive, but he was still cut to the quick. One of the pieces of shrapnel had gone right to the bone, shredding his flesh like paper. Shredding everything he was in the process.

As he felt a puff of Kin's breath, and then warm lips against the top of his spine, Jack shuddered and made a high-pitched sound that could only be called a whimper. Jack knew what Kin was seeing—the raised bumps of ripped flesh and burned skin that would never heal properly, snaking down from his neck and across his right shoulder blade all the way down below his waistband.

His ears buzzed like the droning of bees, and his nostrils were singed with acrid smoke. There were ashes and sand in his mouth, and he was choking on it. The pain was red hot, and this was it—he was going to die. Fuck, he was dying, and it hurt so much that it should be a relief, but he didn't want to die, and he screamed, but there was only buzzing. Then Sagemiller was there, his lips moving, but no sound coming out. He was dragging Jack across the burning tarmac, and Jesus, where was Grant?

He gasped, and Kin wrapped his arms around him, his lips a whisper across Jack's neck and shoulder.

"I've got you."

Tears pricked at his eyes, and Jack took a deep breath as he sagged back against Kin. "Please. I need...I just..." What? What did he need? He wasn't sure.

But Kin somehow seemed to understand, and he guided Jack to the empty bed, stripping off the rest of Jack's clothes and sitting him on the side and urging him onto his back, keeping his hips by the edge.

Naked but for the tensor bandage around his sore knee, Jack parted his legs, and Kin kneeled between them. Jack propped himself on his elbows and watched, shivering as Kin ran his palms along Jack's inner thighs, his lips parted and eyes bright.

He protested when Kin moved away, but Kin was only propping pillows behind Jack so he could watch without straining. Jack settled back with a sigh as Kin kneeled between his thighs again. It was a glorious sight to see.

Jack's cock was half hard, curving to his belly. With a small smile, Kin kissed the tip of it, and then explored the thatch of Jack's pubic hair, barely touching him, but sending shocks of pleasure across his skin. The pink-burgundy duvet was cheap but soft, and Jack squirmed on it, lifting his hips with a groan.

But Kin seemed determined to torture him, and what exquisite torment it was—every bit as good as he'd imagined in that night in the tent when Kin sucked his cold fingers. Kin's tongue was rough and wet along the smooth skin of Jack's inner thighs and belly, and Jack was quivering by the time Kin lapped at his balls and his hole, pressing his legs back carefully, clearly mindful of Jack's injuries.

As the pleasure built, Jack didn't feel any pain, and there was something glorious about being splayed so wantonly with Kin kneeling before him still fully dressed in his uniform. Jack had never spread himself open for Grant like this. It had always been hurried, and Jack had never let Grant fuck him. But now he wished Kin would, even if it would be too much for Jack's shoulder and knee.

Kin had seen his scars—kissed them even—and somehow he still wanted him. Jack felt as though something hard that had been lodged in his chest had gone soft and drained away. He reached a hand for Kin's thick, dark hair, caressing his head as Kin got him harder and harder without touching his cock.

When he finally took Jack in his mouth, sucking him almost to the root with a sure movement, Jack arched his back, his cry echoing through the room.

Kin's hand clapped over Jack's mouth, and he pulled off. "Shh. Thin walls."

Then the hot suction of his mouth enveloped Jack again, and Jack moaned loudly, muffled by Kin's palm. He thrust his hips up as need built in him, thick and powerful.

Having Kin's hand over his mouth somehow made it even better, and he gripped Kin's wrist, groaning and closing his eyes to the pink-beige ceiling. He was pinned, Kin sucking him fiercely, and Jack had never felt so free.

He practically levitated off the bed when he came hard. With each hot pulse, the intensity of his release grew, and he gasped against Kin's hand, shaking as Kin milked him, swallowing repeatedly.

When Kin pulled off, he licked his lips, catching the semen dripping down his chin. He met Jack's gaze and smiled, lifting his hand from Jack's mouth. He drew circles on Jack's thighs.

"Sorry. It's just that if someone heard us…"

Jack pushed himself up, shaking his head. "No, I…" He returned Kin's smile. "I liked it. I liked it like that."

"Yeah?" Kin smiled wickedly. "Good to know." Running a hand through his hair, Kin got to his feet. "I guess we should…"

"Get you off? Yes, we should." Jack reached for Kin's uniform pants and tugged them down his hips, along with his briefs. Kin was hard and leaking, and Jack didn't have it in him to tease, instead wasting no time in sucking him.

Kin wove his fingers into Jack's hair, murmuring something in Inuktitut. Jack didn't know the words, but he understood all the same.

Chapter Seven

I T HAD BEEN dark for hours by the time they made it to Nanisivik, the stars glittering and the moon standing sentry. Kin smiled to himself as Jack turned in a circle on the snow-dusted oval concrete jetty, his head tipped back. The hood of his parka slipped back off his toque.

"Look at Ursa Major. Everything seems closer somehow."

Kin kept his gaze on Jack. He'd seen the stars a million times, and this would likely be his last chance to see this man. The morning would come all too soon, and Jack would return to Ottawa and his life. Kin wished he could ignore the ache that accompanied the thought. *We just met. I should just be glad I got some action for a change. It was fun while it lasted.*

But it wasn't. It wasn't *fun*. And the emotions he'd experienced having sex with Jack weren't what he'd felt in the past getting laid. Even now, his stomach fluttered, and he wanted to drag Jack close and kiss him until they couldn't breathe. He wanted to get him naked again, and fuck him senseless. He wanted to see him peaceful after an orgasm, the wrinkles in his forehead temporarily smoothed away, and his jaw slack.

"What were the stars like in the desert?"

Eyes on the sky, Jack smiled sadly. "It was my favorite part of being there. The sky was so dark, and if there were clouds, they looked like black holes in the sea of stars. Parts of the Milky Way actually cast shadows on the ground at times. And in late winter there was the zodiacal light."

"What's that?" He liked watching Jack talk about astronomy. It brought a peace to his expression that Kin felt mirrored inside.

"About an hour and a half after sunset, a faint glow would reach up from the western horizon. It was like a huge slanted pyramid of yellow light, and sometimes it would stretch so high. It's caused by sunlight reflecting off meteoric dust. Can't compare to the northern lights, but it was beautiful all the same. Grant said once—" He broke off, swallowing hard. "He said it looked like the path to heaven. Then he laughed, and said the dust was affecting his brain."

Kin waited silently, tamping down the immediate flare of unfair jealousy. Jack still stared at the stars, and was quiet for a minute before he spoke again.

"Going out there that day, it was recce by death, you know?"

"I'm not sure I do," Kin said quietly.

"Sorry. Reconnaissance by death. Like reconnaissance by fire, but worse. We'd go into the desert in a few G-Wagons, and there was no protection if you got hit. If someone ahead doesn't report back once they go over a hill, and then there's smoke rising, it's a good bet the enemy's over there. Not the kind of recon anyone wants to do. We were in the lead vehicle, and there was a kid up ahead on the road. A little girl."

Kin's gut twisted.

"I had to send Grant. I couldn't play favorites, or make it seem like I was. I had to be fair."

"Of course."

Jack's breath hitched, and he dropped his eyes to the horizon, his gaze distant. "I'd known him for years. He was a good man. We'd hooked up on leave when we got the chance. We never snuck around while we were on duty. That was a strict rule. We were both officers, and then he became my lieutenant. It had always been casual until then."

"And then it wasn't?"

"Grant wanted more. We knew the mission in Afghanistan was wrapping up, and we were starting to think about life back home, or on a base somewhere like Germany. Grant wanted to move in together. He...he said he loved me." Jack shook his head. "But the thing is…I didn't love him." As the words came out in a puff of frozen breath, he shuddered. "I wanted to love him," he whispered. "But I didn't."

Kin took a step toward him. He hated seeing the torment that creased Jack's face, and wanted to hold him and kiss him until it disappeared. But he stopped an arm's length away. If Jack needed to talk, he would listen.

"The worst part is that he knew it." Jack's eyes shone in the starlight, the nearly full moon rising above him. "I liked him. I really did. But it wasn't enough. I didn't want to live with him, and I didn't have the guts to tell him. He was from Toronto, and he'd talk about moving to Ottawa, and I'd nod and smile, and hope that he'd change his mind. Then I sent him onto that road and got him killed."

"No. It wasn't your fault."

Jack swung around to look at Kin now. "How do you know? You weren't there. I should have sent the new guy, or I should have gone myself."

"I know because it was war. Because you didn't plant the bomb. You were doing your job. It wasn't your fault. And you almost got killed yourself." He thought of the scars on Jack's back, and wanted to kiss them all again.

"I went after him. I could hear the little girl wailing." He squeezed his eyes shut. "I can still hear her. Then there was nothing but burning."

Kin did take Jack in his arms then, holding him close and wishing there were no winter layers between them.

Jack's voice was muffled against Kin's shoulder. "I woke up in the hospital, and I knew he was dead. They didn't have to tell me. His mother wrote me, saying how happy I'd made him, and she was glad he'd had me there with him." He shook, and his voice broke. "But I didn't love him, Kin. I didn't."

"It's okay." He murmured little Inuktitut lullabies, rubbing Jack's back.

Even when Jack finally stopped trembling, Kin still soothed him, wishing he could take all the pain away forever. He thought of his brother, and fought the lump that formed in his throat. Sniffing, Jack raised his head. His eyes were red and wet, but he managed a little smile.

"I've never told anyone that. I think you've cast a spell on me. Thank you."

Kin brushed Jack's cheeks dry with his glove. "For what?"

"Everything. For listening. For…being you." He took a deep breath. "I've been going through the motions for a long time. You changed that. This place changed that."

Kin reached for him, wanting to kiss him again and again, but Jack stepped back. Kin dropped his arm and tried not to feel hurt.

Jack cleared his throat. "So, this is Nanisivik."

"Yes." Kin tamped down the disappointment. It was back to business, and it was for the best. *He's leaving. Don't get attached.* Of course it was far too late for that, but that was his problem. He kept his voice even. "This is it."

Aside from the concrete jetty, all that was left of the old mine was a small tank farm where several large cylinders of fuel for the navy ships were stored. The land was rocky, all dirt and stone beneath the drifts of snow. The wind was quiet, providing a respite from the biting cold. The ice was forming on the water, and soon it would be completely covered.

Sniffing, Jack smirked at the battered, weather-beaten government sign nearby on the jetty, which had been triumphantly unveiled by the prime minister years ago during a visit. It read in English and French: *Future Site of Canada's Arctic Deep Water Port.*

"Or not, as the case may be," Jack said.

"They said it was too expensive to construct a full base in the permafrost north of the Arctic Circle." Kin tugged on his red toque where it had started to ride up over his earlobe. Apparently they didn't realize where Nanisivik was when they made the plans."

Jack chuckled. "Apparently not. It happens— places move around. It's very confusing for the government." He gazed around. "I think this is…"

"Desolate? Depressing?" Kin suggested. He tried

to keep his tone light. He loved his home, and it was understandable that Jack wouldn't.

"Perfect."

Kin blinked. "Huh?"

Jack took a deep breath. "I said it's perfect. I spoke to Colonel Fournier this morning. Etienne. He's been a friend for a long time. Anyway, I told him we need to establish a training center here. Our soldiers can learn so much in the Arctic. We're protecting a country with a massive amount of land in the north, and we're not prepared. We need to be. Training missions, drills, search and rescue—we can do it all here. There's a port to bring in supplies, and a road to Arctic Bay. We could work with the community. Use your expertise. Provide jobs. But we'd be far enough away that it wouldn't impact daily life. It would—" He broke off. "Well, what do you think?"

Kin's heart was beating double time. "You'd consult the council on the plans?"

"Yes. On everything. I'd want full cooperation with the community. Make it a partnership. Fournier agrees. We'd get your help in building the dorms and the admin buildings. Use the same prefabs you have in Arctic Bay. We'd keep it small. The idea is that we'd be training out on the land most of the time. I'd need an office and—"

"You?" Kin's mouth was dry. Were his ears playing tricks?

Jack smiled tentatively. "I'd be the commander."

"The commander," Kin repeated. He tingled all over.

Jack's smile faded. "Well, nothing's confirmed yet. The colonel was enthusiastic, and he thinks he can get the go-ahead by December for me to come back and start planning. He was happy to hear me excited about something again. Since I came home, it's like…like I've been frozen. But now I'm feeling again. Thawing out, I guess. Which is all ironic and whatever since it happened in the Arctic."

Kin chuckled. "Alanis Morissette should write a song about it."

"I haven't been able to connect with anyone in so long. Just Neville, but he's easy."

Kin's gut tightened. "Neville?" The name was familiar, but his spinning mind couldn't place it.

Jack regarded him seriously. "Yeah. He sleeps with me most nights. Incredibly loyal. Enjoys licking me. Drools a lot, but it works for him. I'd be bringing him with me when I come back."

The tension evaporated as quickly as it had come. "Hmm. So you're looking for a threesome?"

"Absolutely. Pugs make great thirds, or so I'm told."

"I guess I'm open to some kink," Kin said, laughing.

Jack regarded him intently. "But in all seriousness, it wouldn't have to be me commanding the training base. Either way I think the project is important."

"But it does." Kin closed the few feet between them. "It has to be you."

The lines around Jack's eyes crinkled as he grinned. "You'd want that? You'd want…me?"

He didn't hesitate. "Yes." He could hardly believe this was happening. "You'd really want to stay?"

Nodding, Jack brushed their dry lips together and ran his gloved hands up and down Kin's arms. "I didn't want to come here. I didn't want to be anywhere. Then it all changed. I met you, and…and I don't understand what it is about this place. It's fucking freezing, and dark, and a million miles from anything, and somehow I don't want to leave." He laughed. "I really don't want to leave, Kin."

Kin's heart soared. "Then don't. I mean, I know you have to go back to Ottawa first, but…come back."

"I will. I know it's only been a few days, and I'm not expecting anything. This is all new. But when I'm with you, I feel…I feel *good*. Whole again in a way I can't explain. Is that crazy?"

"If it is, I'm crazy too." Kin took Jack's face in his hands. "I want to know you—every little last thing."

They kissed on the old jetty under the stars with icebergs standing watch, heat flaring between them like the puffs of their breath in the Arctic air. Jack's mouth was wet and warm, and Kin never wanted to stop kissing him.

An insistent little voice reminded him that it wouldn't be easy. They barely knew each other, and how would he keep it a secret from his family and the community? Could they hide it? *Do I really want to?*

But he pushed the worries away as Jack pressed his nose and lips against Kin's cheek in a kunik, inhaling deeply. Kin held Jack fiercely. They'd cross those bridges soon enough. Tonight, all that mattered was that they were together.

Tonight, he was falling in love with Captain Jack Turner.

THE END

About the Author

After writing for years yet never really finding the right inspiration, Keira discovered her voice in gay romance, which has become a passion. She writes contemporary, historical, paranormal, and fantasy fiction, and—although she loves delicious angst along the way—Keira firmly believes in happy endings. For as Oscar Wilde once said, "The good ended happily, and the bad unhappily. That is what fiction means."

Find out more about Keira's books and sign up for her monthly gay romance e-newsletter:

keiraandrews.com